Lord

of the

Underworld

Curse of the Gods book 4

by Danielle James

Ἄδης

Περσεφόνη

Prologue

Many eons ago, the Creator, the one true God, created all that is. He created the universe, the stars, and the planets. He created the plants and water on those worlds. He created realms and different planes of existence. Yet, there was something missing. That was when He created life-forms. Not only did He create humans, but Fae, shifters, elves, gnomes, sprites, nymphs, and many,

many more. He gifted some of these beings with special magic that would ensure that every species lived in harmony and that this world, this entity that He created, would survive.

Knowing that this thing He had created would need constant love and attention, He created beings to assist Him. Lesser gods and goddesses to watch over His wondrous creation. He gifted them, as well, with the power to influence things such as love, fertility, war, and peace. He loved these gods and goddesses so much, that He gifted them with their most prized possession: free will.

For a time, everything worked in complete melodiousness; everyone did their jobs, and all living things were exultant.

But that was not to remain.

The gods and goddesses became different over time. The entities that resided on the sky mountain, Olympus in particular, changed. They had become selfish, petty, and cruel. Some interfered in the lives of humans for their own entertainment and not for the greater good. This was not what they had been created to be, and their actions and self-importance became so atrocious that the Creator knew He had to do something. Unwilling to destroy his beloved—albeit misguided—gods and goddesses, He imprisoned them all with a curse, each unique to the deity that it confined. The curses were meant to be broken, of course, but only when the cursed learned the lesson the Creator intended…

Chapter One

Persephone, Goddess of Spring, held the brown and yellow leaf in her hand before letting it fall to the ground. Her time on Earth was getting shorter with each passing day. Already, she could feel the pull of the Underworld calling to her, forcing her to eventually go there against her will. It broke her heart each autumn when her beautiful creations withered and died, and even though she knew she would return in six months to see it back to full beauty once again, she hated the time in between.

Hades had been known as a horrible god to everyone else, and when they had been cursed to marry and she to be with him six months out of the year, she had believed so as well. Over the centuries, Persephone had learned to love him, and eventually, given into her desire to be close to him. Sex was one of their best activities, and it seemed the only time he was truly interested in her.

Contrary to popular belief, Hades had never taken her against her will. He only came to her when she called for him, the rest of the time he maintained his distance.

Her heart yearned for him to love her as much as she loved him, but she knew it was not to be. He wasn't as bad as others believed, but he did not love her. This she knew. Hades was just like all the other gods: selfish and petty, even cruel at times. As she admired one of the final blooms on a rose bush, she subconsciously placed her hand over her belly. She had to protect her heart from him, and now, she had a life growing inside of her that must be protected, as well.

The urge to return to the Underworld was strong, but Persephone knew she could not go. But how? What would become of her if she did not? And what of her baby?

She thought this over all spring and summer, but nothing came to her that would help. If the child were born in the Underworld, she would be condemned to stay there, born into the curse. But if she could just hold on a little longer, her child would be free.

She used the last of her waning power to ghost herself to the only other person who might be able to help. Her mother.

***

Hades hated the day that Persephone, his wife, was to return to the Underworld. It was a constant reminder of his curse, of his imprisonment to never be with another. She would return, and he would lay eyes upon her. He would be able to feel her watching him, although she'd never judged him. She would be there. He'd be able to smell her, to hear her in her wing of the palace, hear her voice. It pissed him off, not because all of those things would happen, but that he looked forward to it. He would never admit it aloud, or even to himself, but he missed her when she was gone. The Lord of the Underworld looked forward to the day she would return. Time crawled at a snail's pace when she was gone. Food lost its appeal. He didn't even enjoy smiting those in Tartarus when Persephone wasn't around. It was as if she provided some measure of completeness, which was ridiculous. Hades didn't need anyone.

He repeated this thought to himself over and over again as he paced the length of his throne room. He did not want nor need a wife. Before the curse, Hades had taken his fair share of women and then some. Females bowed to him, begging for his attention. They still did, but he could no longer take them to his bed. Forced or not, marriage was sacred, and Hades would not find himself a prisoner in Tartarus because he couldn't keep his dick in his pants. Not that he wanted anyone else. The first time Persephone had asked him to her bed, he'd known there would never be another.

At one point, while she was topside doing whatever she did for those six months, Hades had been weak. Or stupid. It didn't matter, because when he attempted to entertain another in his chambers, he found that he could not. The female held no interest to him, and he'd sent her away. That damned curse had tied him to the Goddess of Spring in more ways than one.

Glancing at the ornate stone clock over his throne, Hades grumbled to himself. Not only was she ruining his eternity, but she was late in doing so. He ran his hand over his red hair and sat heavily on his throne. Where was she?

"Sir," Hypnos, the God of Night and Sleep, said as he ghosted into the throne room.

"If it's not life or death, I don't care," Hades growled at him.

"I was wondering where I might find Persephone." Hypnos prattled on as though Hades had not said a word.

"You and me both," Hades snarled. "When she arrives, there will be hell to pay."

"She's not here?" Hypnos's eyebrows shot to his hairline.

Hades understood completely. The Goddess of Spring was never late. Ever.

"No," Hades said. "And good riddance."

"Surely you don't mean that." Hypnos suggested. "Maybe she's just delayed. Would you like me to look for her the next time I'm topside?"

Hades glared at the man. His curse was to the Underworld, but at least he was able to leave each night. Hypnos had a job to do on Earth and he *had* to do it. Hades's job, however, was centered in the Underworld and he could not leave. Not even to find his wife. What if she were unable to return? What if someone had done her harm? What if she—no, he couldn't even think it.

"Or not." Hypnos turned to leave.

"You will look for her," Hades snarled.

"Okay, okay." Hypnos held up his hands. "I thought by the way you were growling that you didn't want me to."

"I was *not* growling!" Hades bellowed, his voice echoed off the walls, and the floor vibrated with the timbre. "Get out of my sight."

He watched Hypnos turn to leave. Was that a smile on his face? The God of Sleep had better not have been smiling. How dare he laugh at the Lord of the Underworld? How dare he mock his king? Just as soon as he found Persephone, Hypnos was going to meet an untimely demise, Hades decided. *Ungrateful wretch*, he thought. *It's time he learned a lesson. But first, Persephone.*

It wasn't like she could choose to stay away. The curse forced her to return at the end of each summer. Even if she could fight the pull of the curse, her powers would weaken until they disappeared altogether, leaving her a mere mortal. No, she wouldn't stay away by choice. Something must have happened to her. She must be a prisoner somewhere.

But who would want to harm Persephone? She was the epitome of all that was good and right in the world. She was pure of heart, loving and forgiving. She held grudges against no one and didn't judge anyone, not even Hades. No matter how much of a bastard he was, his goddess stood by his side, loyal even to a fault.

Hades, however, had many enemies. It would not surprise him in the least if someone had taken issue with him and was trying to use Persephone to get to him. Well, it wasn't going to work. Hades loved no one. Perhaps if they killed the goddess, his curse would be broken, and he could go on about his eternity in peace.

The thought left a bad taste in his mouth and caused his stomach to tie itself into a knot. Persephone was his and he could not allow any harm to come to her. He couldn't afford to wait for Hypnos to find her. Pushing to his feet, Hades knew what he had to do.

He attempted to ghost out of the Underworld but was hit with what felt like a brick wall. He'd expected that. When the curse had originally been cast, he'd tried to get out repeatedly. Every time he was met with that invisible wall. He could ghost himself freely within the confines of the Underworld, but no farther. *Fine*, he thought.

With only a thought, Hades was standing on the dock of the River Styx.

"Hades," Charon, the ferryman, greeted him with a bow of his head. "How can I be of assistance?"

"Take me across," Hades commanded.

Charon shook his hooded head. "You know that I cannot."

"You will do as I say!" Hades bellowed.

"It isn't that I do not want to help you, it's that the curse will not allow you on my gondola."

"This is bullshit." Hades tried to jump on the gondola, but before his feet could touch the tiny craft, he was suddenly thrown back on his ass and onto the rocky shore. He jerked his head up to see Charon attempting to cover his laughter. Growling, Hades glared at the ferryman.

"What?" Charon said, pulling his hood down lower to cover his face. "I told you so."

Hades opened his mouth to chastise him, but he was suddenly overwhelmed with emotion. Flashes of pain and anguish sliced through his chest, and he began to feel remorse, worry, and real fear for his wife. The waters of the river had touched his feet, causing the angst.

Rubbing his chest, Hades jumped to his feet, glaring at the ferryman. "Fuck you, Charon." He turned on his heel, grumbling under his breath, "Fuck that torturous boat, fuck that river, and fuck this godforsaken curse!"

Chapter Two

"How did you get here?" Demeter asked as her daughter appeared in front of her. Persephone was one of the very few deities who knew to find her in the gardens after dinner. "How did you get past the dragon?"

"The dragon has no qualm with me," Persephone answered. "She's quite friendly, actually." The three-headed dragon that guarded the entrance to Olympus not only saw that enemies did not enter, but that the gods cursed to the sky mountain did not leave. The Goddess of Spring, however, had a different kind of curse.

"The solstice has passed," her mother said. "Aren't you supposed to be in the Underworld now?"

Persephone felt an increase in the pull to return just at hearing the name of her prison. Subconsciously, her eyes cut downward, as if hell itself would rise up to retrieve her. "Yes. But I can't go back there."

Demeter gazed at her with sympathy in her eyes. She hated that. She didn't need her mother to feel sorry for her, she needed her mother's help. "I need you to cloak me. I need you to hide me from my curse."

Her mother's brows scrunched together, and her mouth turned down into a frown. "You know I can't do that. I couldn't shield you anymore than you could do it yourself. It would only last for a short time. One season, if we're lucky. Has that man done something to you?"

"I can't shield myself at all," Persephone said. "And no, Hades is always good to me. At least, as much as he is capable of. He's never hurt me."

"Then go back," Demeter said. "Go back. Recharge your powers, and then next year, you can shield yourself."

Persephone shook her head. "If only I could." She pulled her robe open, allowing it to fall from her shoulders, and exposing her rounded belly. "I don't want this life for my young."

"How many months?" Demeter moved closer and rested her hand on Persephone's stomach.

"Seven," she said. "Mother, you know that if she is born in the Underworld, she will bear a curse she did not earn."

"I do know this," Demeter replied. "I can protect you, but only until the baby is born. What will you do then?"

"I'll return to my place at the palace with Hades."

"And the child?"

A deep sorrow filled her chest and tears stung at her eyes. "I will have to entrust her to someone who can give her a good life." She paused for a moment. "A good, human life."

"Does Hades know?"

Persephone shook her head. "He doesn't know how to love. I want my baby to be loved."

Her mother folded her arms around Persephone and embraced her tight. "Doing what is right and what is best for your child is not always the easiest path."

Tears that she'd held back for weeks spilled over, and she cried into her mother's embrace. "Please help me."

"I will use all the magic I can to shield you from the curse, and from Hades. It will only last until the new year begins. It will not take long for the curse to drain you of your power. Save what you can, use it only in emergencies."

She sniffled. "Thank you."

"You know that if your power is depleted while on Earth, you will become mortal," her mother reminded her in a serious tone. "You cannot get them back."

"If I could stay with my child where she and I could be mortal, that would be the perfect life," Persephone said, already wishing for it with all her heart, also knowing it was not to be, nor was she being entirely honest. The perfect life would be one free of the curse, one in which Hades loved her as she did him, and that he would love their child unconditionally. The perfect life would be the three of them, living as a family.

It would never be perfect, but she would have the knowledge that her child was safe, and she'd done all she could to get her there.

Demeter held her daughter out at arm's length and called upon her magic. The air sizzled with the goddess's power and a gentle breeze blew, wrapping around Persephone's body. Then it dissipated as quickly as it had begun.

"You are now shielded from the curse and from Hades. I will send you to a place where you'll be safe."

"Thank you, Mother," Persephone said sincerely. She wrapped her arms around herself as her mother used her own power to send her to Earth.

***

When Persephone opened her eyes, she found herself standing in a crowded park. Humans surrounded her, bustling along their way, never once noticing a pregnant woman who just appeared out of thin air. Humans had become so jaded, so blind over the centuries that even when something was obviously different, they took no notice of it. Everyone had their noses in their phones or tablets. No one took the time to just sit and watch the world go by.

It broke her heart. She worked all season to bring the beauty of spring to mortals and no one even looked up anymore. No one noticed how many colors decorated a single flower. No one noticed the way the birds flocked to the trees to build their summer homes as soon as the leaves began to bud. No one realized that every detail of the spring and summer were planned out in an intricate web of cause and effect and that everything had its purpose, even the falling of the leaves.

Yes, it left the trees bare. Yes, the flowers died or went into hibernation, and yes, all of her beautiful creations were lost to the harsh cold of winter. But where her magic ended, another began. Skadi, the Norse Goddess of Winter, picked up where Persephone left off each year. She chilled the air and brought the snow and ice, decorating the world in a white and silvery blanket of wonder and awe.

Not that the humans appreciated any of it. Instead, they complained about how cold it was and how they had to shovel the snow to get into their cars. The same with summer. It was too hot. Too much rain. Too much this, or too much that. Humans were insufferable. And yet, here she was, hoping against all the odds that her child would be born a human.

Persephone knew she would have to walk away when the child was born. She knew her purpose was to bring on the spring and give the earth life once again. Without her power, the world would wither away and die like a cold, dead stone, floating aimlessly through the universe.

Wrapping her arms around her belly, Persephone fought back tears. She would leave her. But not yet. She would find a safe place to bring the child into the world, and when it was done, she would go back to her place with Hades in Hell.

***

"What do you want?" Hades growled from his seat on the throne.

"Something has happened," Thanatos told him.

"You've found Persephone?" Hades leaned forward so that the light touched his face, hating the anticipation and hope that grew inside of him.

Thanatos shook his head. "I'm afraid not. Loki is loose on Earth and he let all of the gods on Olympus free."

"All of them?" Hades asked. "How?" If Loki was running amok, then he needed to act quickly. The trickster had a "devil may care" attitude, but Hades knew that the Norse god was lethal.

"Put the dragon to sleep," Thanatos said. "They all escaped." Hades knew that the god was waiting for the Lord of the

Underworld to roar, to bitch to the heavens for some kind of trademark explosion, but that wasn't what Hades wanted right then. He just waited for the God of Death to continue. "I'm on a quest to find the ones I can."

That's what he needed. He needed out of the Underworld. "I will go with you." Hades leaned forward, a plan forming in his mind.

"You can't leave here," Thanatos reminded him. "How will you get out?"

"You must go to Olympus. I need Aphrodite's cloak." With the cloak, Hades could hide from the ferryman; he could hide from the curse just long enough to get out.

"What good is that old horse blanket gonna do you in here?" Thanatos raised one of his dark brows in question.

He should smite the SOB on principle. How dare he question Hades? No. Smiting would do no good in getting his ass out of the Underworld. He could kick the God of Death's ass later. After he found his wife. "With the cloak," Hades ground out while gritting his teeth, "and my helmet, I

24

could provide enough shielding to slip past the ferryman and out of this place. I can get free and find"—He almost said Persephone, but quickly rearranged his speech—"the other gods. You need all the help you can get."

Thanatos didn't look like he believed him. "And what about Persephone?" That shit always cut right to the heart of the matter. Hades would be smiting his smartass, just not yet.

"I hope to find her as well, but she is a goddess," Hades said, trying to keep his cool. "As far as we know, she's galivanting about with the rest of them, living it up somewhere while I sit down here and rot."

Thanatos appeared wary for a moment, and then ghosted out of the Underworld. Hades knew he'd only be gone for a matter of minutes, so the god ghosted himself to his own chambers to gather a few personal items. His Helm of Darkness, which had been a gift from the Hecatoncheires and the Elder Cyclopes, the very first of their race, forged as a gift in exchange for their freedom so long ago, now would be a pivotal key in Hades's freedom.

Ghosting back to the throne room, Hades waited for Thanatos to return. As expected, it wasn't long. The god ghosted back in with the royal-blue cloak draped over his arm.

"I knew there was a reason I hadn't locked you in Tartarus," Hades said, taking the cloak from him. He wrapped it around his massive shoulders, after grabbing his Helm of Darkness, and disappeared. "Let's go."

Thanatos placed a hand on Hades's shoulder and ghosted them both out of the Underworld. Once outside, he let Hades go. Removing the cloak and Helm, he became visible once again. "Thank you," he said sincerely. Thanatos had done Hades a great service. He would wait to smite him until a later date. He had more pressing matters to handle, anyway. "Now, if you'll excuse me, I have a wife to find."

"Hades, wait!" Thanatos shouted to the god's retreating back.

Hades did not need, nor did he care what further blather the God of Death had to impart with. It was likely something along the lines of, "Help us find the gods, do this, do that, me, me, us... whine, bitch, moan..." There was no time for that when Persephone was out there unprotected. When the god kept talking, Hades ghosted himself away.

Chapter Three

Hades could feel the power of Olympus from a city in the desert. It was pulsing, beckoning him to come to it. Persephone must be there. That was where he needed to go. When he left Thanatos outside of the cavern, he aimed for that power.

When he appeared in that location, Hades couldn't believe what he was seeing. Even though it was night, the human streets were lit by thousands of lights shining from every building. They were illuminated in every color, some flashing, some even blinking in a fashion that seemed like one light was chasing another. People lined the streets, talking, drinking, and having a good time. He must have ghosted into a festival of some sort.

He began walking, still feeling the pull of power, stepping onto the street. A blaring sound caused him to look up just in time to see a metal box on wheels screech by him.

"What the—" Hades jumped back onto the curb quickly.

There were many of those moving boxes. He watched as people got into them and then began moving. Chariots. They were chariots. He needed to get one of those. A man wearing purple dress pants and a suit jacket caught his attention. He was standing with his hip leaned against a sleek, black chariot.

"You there," Hades demanded, pointing at the man. "Is this your chariot?"

The man stared at him like he'd grown another head, then a smile spread across his face. "You with one of the shows?" he asked around a lit cigarette in his mouth.

"No. I am in search of a formidable chariot. This one looks sufficient."

"You bet she is." The man ran his hand over the hood. "She's a 2019 Charger, got an eight-cylinder Jasper engine, double Harvey's and duel exhaust. Packing about four hundred horses under the hood. She can go from zero to sixty in six seconds flat."

Hades looked at the odd machine. How did they get that many horses under the hood? Whatever, it didn't matter. "You will give it to me."

The man chuckled without a bit of mirth in his tone. "Or, you can keep your crazy ass away from my baby, and I'll let you live."

Hades growled and used his powers on the man to bend his will. "You will give it to me," he repeated.

"Look, buddy, I didn't come here lookin' for trouble, but I tell you what, you keep at it and there's gonna be trouble."

Why wasn't it working? Why wouldn't the human do what he said?

"Never mind him." A female voice sounded from behind him. Hades turned to look at her. She had blonde hair that was sticking out around her head like a cloud of golden curls, a leather bustier, and a short skirt. "He's on his period. Maybe I can help you?" She accented her offer with a touch of her hand on Hades's chest.

"I'm looking for my wife." Hades shrugged away from the woman. He didn't like the way it made him feel when she touched him. It made him feel *dirty*. "She is Persephone, the Goddess of Spring, and I must locate her." His chest puffed out just a bit as he named his wife, feeling the pride well up inside of him.

"If it's a goddess you're looking for, you should try Caesar's Palace," she said. "It's only a few blocks ahead."

Hades nodded. Caesar's Palace did seem like a place where gods and goddesses would go. He stomped off in the direction the woman indicated. It didn't take him long to find it, either. There was a flashing light in front of it saying just that.

Why did the humans build a monument to Caesar? That fucker had been dead for centuries. He'd been a son of a bitch in life and did not deserve a monument. Hades shook his head. He would never fully understand humans. It didn't matter. He wasn't there for the humans. He wanted to find his wife.

Stomping to the entrance, Hades growled at the guard. The man, of course, recognized Hades's raw, god powers and stepped aside, allowing the Lord of the Underworld inside. Smart move, lest the man become a resident in the Elysian Fields much sooner than anticipated. It was easy to zero in on the power of Olympus, and that's where he headed.

This palace was unlike anything Hades had ever seen before. People, humans, were everywhere. Each room he passed was filled with humans, playing games of chance, gambling with their riches. Noisy machines lined the walls, beeping and dinging loudly. It was complete chaos. Caesar would be disgusted with this blatant display of disrespect, which was perfect in Hades's eyes. Damned fool.

A dreadful feeling of happiness and well-being washed over him, and Hades turned sharply to his right. Fucking Apollo. The Sun God had that effect on people and gods alike. He was near. Perhaps he'd seen Persephone. Hades scanned the crowd for the tell-tale bleach-blond hair but didn't see it. In fact, all he saw were women, clamoring near a stage where an entertainer wearing only his skivvies was dancing. When the dancer raised his head, Hades rolled his eyes. Fucking Sun God.

"Apollo!" He bellowed over the loud music and the squeals of the females.

The god's eyes shot right to Hades and his brows rose in recognition. A wicked smile spread across his face, and Hades groaned. "Well, look what the cat dragged in." The Sun God announced into a microphone. "It's my brother from another mother, the Lord of the Underworld himself. Escaped from his realm to come party with us! Take a long look, ladies. This ginger is hot, hot, hot!"

Hades was already backing up when the horde of females turned to look at him. He wasn't so sure about this situation at all. They stared at him not as a god worthy of respect, but as a piece of meat, a sex toy meant for their pleasure. His skin began to crawl as they rushed for him like a single unit of sex-starved zombies on the hunt.

Hands touched him. Someone grabbed a hand full of his ass. They were everywhere! Someone was slinking their hand up his battle gear on his thigh. "Ho-no. Stop that!" Hades shouted, but no one listened.

"Now, now, ladies, you know the rules. Lookie, but no touchie," Apollo said into the microphone. "You wouldn't want to have to be punished, would you?" When the women erupted in cheers and applause, Apollo grinned. "You're a bunch of *bad* girls."

Hades glared at Apollo. He would pay for this, but first, he needed an escape. With a tremendous roar, Hades pushed his way through the females to go back out the way he came. Once he was out of that room, he tried to collect himself. What in the ever-loving fuck was the Sun God doing entertaining a bunch of horny females? Had their men gone soft? Were they unable to fulfill their manly duties? What would cause these women to gather and hunt for a mate at a place like this?

"They're here to enjoy themselves," a familiar female voice said.

Hades turned to see Aphrodite sprawled on a chaise lounge chair, while a young human male fed her from a silver tray of grapes and cheese.

"Aphrodite," he growled.

"Yes," she answered with a flourish of her hand. "You're looking like you were hit by a bus. And is that my cloak?"

Hades straightened his spine. "I am searching for Persephone. Have you seen her?"

The Goddess of Love tossed her head back and laughed. "So, the Goddess of Spring has finally had enough of your overbearing, caveman ways and left your sorry ass."

"She is missing," he growled. She would not leave him. She couldn't. It wasn't possible.

"Have you asked Ares?"

"What would the God of War know of my wife?" Hades shouted.

"Well, he *did* break his curse." She shrugged one shoulder. "He's in New York City."

If Ares's curse was broken, he would have all of his powers and be free to roam as he pleased again. That could be useful. Plus, Ares had been on Earth for many years. He would be familiar with modern humans. "How do I find him?" Hades demanded.

"Why don't you just call him," she suggested as if it were that simple.

Hades looked to the sky and yelled, "Ares, you twisted son of a bitch, get your ass over here."

Aphrodite laughed. "That's one way to do it, or you could call him on a cell phone." She lifted a square device that was covered in false diamonds and dangled it in his face. The box made a chiming noise and then lit up.

Hades swatted it out of her hand, slamming it into the wall. "Don't dangle your magical trinkets in my face!"

"You *jerk*. You broke my phone!"

"Ares! Where *is* he?"

"Fuck off," Aphrodite snarled at him while she scampered to pick up the pieces of her trinket. "And give me my cloak back, *asshole*."

Hades walked away, pretending not to hear her as her cloak swayed back and forth from his belt. No way in hell was he giving it back.

"Hey, what a great costume," a male said, touching Hades's shoulder armor. "What show are you with?"

Anger boiled up inside of Hades. He wasn't with a show. He wasn't a plaything for misguided females, and he wasn't a fool. The anger turned to fury and his hair burst into flames as he leaned forward to growl at the human.

The man stared at him in shock for a moment, and then a wide smile spread across his face. "That. Is. Awesome!" He ran off, calling for his friends, no doubt to show them Hades and his wonderful parlor tricks that had no effect on humans. Crushing the feeling of inadequacy he was experiencing, he donned his helmet and then tossed the cloak around his shoulders. He had to get out of there before he did something the world would not soon forget, and he would quite probably be remiss about.

Chapter Four

It hadn't taken Persephone long to realize that her mother had dropped her into the middle of Central Park, New York City. She was familiar with the ways of humans, having been around them as they grew throughout the centuries, so she understood that she couldn't hide in the park for months.

She'd left the park and set out to find herself a suitable place to live. There was a small apartment open only blocks from the park, and the owner was willing to rent monthly on a cash basis. When Persephone opened her bag to pay him, she realized that her mother had filled it with crisp, one-hundred-dollar bills. It was more than enough to provide for herself for the time she needed.

Her powers were kept under lock and key, but she could feel them waning with each passing day. The pull to return to the Underworld had been diminished by her mother's magic, but it was growing stronger once again. Her mother's protection spell was growing weaker, the curse growing stronger with each minute that she spent on Earth.

She'd lasted this long, she decided as she subconsciously rubbed her swollen belly, *she could last just a few more weeks*. The urge to eat human food had become overwhelming, to the point of necessity, so every day Persephone walked to the nearby grocery store. She only picked up what she would need for the day, but each day she bought something for the baby. Sometimes it was diapers, sometimes it was a toy, but always something.

On this day, she was walking through the baby aisle, when her eyes caught on the row of baby formula. Her baby would need that. It would have been preferable to nurse the baby as it was intended, but Persephone knew that if she bonded with the child, she would never be able to leave her when the time came. And it would come. Persephone knew it. She would have to return to the Underworld, to her curse, if she were to recharge her power. Persephone didn't care about her power, but she did care about the world, and it was her job to bring it new life each year. Without her magic, her power, winter would never end and eventually all of the life on Earth would die.

She'd rebelled before. Even refused to bring spring to the world. For years, Persephone hid in the shadows of the Underworld, refusing to cooperate with her curse. It had been disastrous. The humans called it the Ice Age. She called it her worst personal failure. She could not allow that to happen again.

As she studied can after can of powdered infant formula, she rubbed her belly. It calmed her, and she believed it calmed the little one as well. As she tossed three different cans into her cart, the reality of what she was facing hit her hard. She had to give up her child. She would give birth and then leave the child with an adoptive family. She would walk away and never look back, praying that her child had a good life. A better life than what she would have trapped in the Underworld by a curse she didn't deserve.

Hot tears stung her eyes as she tossed more cans into her cart. She got at least two of each kind, unsure of what was the best replacement for mother's milk. Those tears spilled over, running down her face in a river as the pain rolled over her. She hated this. In all of her years, Persephone had never hated anyone or anything, not even Hades when they were cursed to be together. She had accepted her fate gracefully and she wasn't even sure she knew how to hate. However, now she knew differently. She hated the circumstances. Hated that damn curse, hated everything about her situation. She didn't want her child to drink formula. She didn't want to live in that tiny apartment, she didn't want to hide, didn't want to return to the Underworld, but most of all, she didn't want to walk away from the most precious life she'd ever created growing inside of her.

She slammed can after can into the cart, uncaring about the tears that streaked her face, or how she could barely breathe through her sobs. She didn't care if anyone saw her, or what they thought. For five weeks she'd lived under the radar, kept her composure, and she was done with that. She was not ready to be separated from her young, and time was growing shorter and shorter.

A strong hand landed gently on her shoulder. "Ma'am?" A man's voice asked from behind her. "I don't know what's happened, but if there is a way I can help, I'm here."

Persephone spun around, forcing his hand off of her. "Unhand me," she snarled. She glared up into the surprised face of the God of War.

His slashing, dark brows were wrinkled in confusion, his eyes narrowed, and his mouth hanging open in shock. "Persephone?"

"Do not say my name," she hissed at him, gaining control of her emotions and straightening her spine.

"What are you doing here?" he asked. "I mean, I knew you were not where you were supposed to be, but in New York? Why?

And does Hades know? What's going on? Did you break your curse?" He paced back and forth in the aisle that was really too small for his massive frame. The way he rubbed his hand over his short hair would have been comical had she not been in the middle of a breakdown.

"It's none of your business," she grumbled, grabbing her cart and shoving it through the aisle.

"Wait," he said, catching up to her quickly and taking her arm.

She turned her head to glare at him. "Take your hand off me."

He released her immediately. "I'm sorry, but I heard you hadn't returned to the Underworld, and now you're here, and *what the fuck is that*?" His voice shot up three octaves as he pointed at her pregnant belly. "Holy shit. This is bad. *Really* bad. How did that happen? I mean, I *know* how that happened, but when? *Who*? What about your powers? You can't use your powers. When is it due?"

Persephone watched as Ares rapid-fired one question after another at her. She didn't bother to try to answer him—she wouldn't have been able to get a word in edgewise. He was working it out in his head, out loud, and she would just have to wait for him to reach the end of his blathering. *Or,* she thought, *she could ghost away.* It would be a gross misuse of what little power she had, but it would get her away from Ares. When she closed her eyes to do just that, Ares took her wrist in his hand.

"No," he said. "I don't know what's going on with you and I don't care. I do know that you can't deplete your powers. The whole fucking world depends on you. You're coming with me."

She bristled. "I most certainly am not." Not even Hades bossed her around anymore. He'd tried, at first, but soon learned that the Goddess of Spring was no spring chicken and could certainly hold her own against a bully.

"I'm sorry, Princess," He rested his palm on her shoulder, "but you are."

Persephone opened her mouth to argue with him, but he'd already ghosted her to another place. This was someone's home, she decided as she took in her surroundings. A long, overstuffed sectional sofa in soft brown material lined two walls of the room she was in. A large television screen was attached to the adjacent wall with a five-shelf bookcase full of books underneath it. In the far corner, a matching recliner and ottoman sat, as if waiting for someone to sit in it.

"Where am I?" Persephone demanded. "You will take me back right now."

Ares shook his head. "I've been around a long time and I know when there's something going on. I also know that if you've found a way to resist returning to the Underworld, and I'm assuming it has something to do with the fact that you're very pregnant, then Hades is probably looking for you. Since no one has seen you for months, that can't be an accident. So, this is the most protected house on Earth. No one gets in without the owner's permission."

"You got in," she pointed out.

"It's *my* house."

"What in the blazes is going on out here?" A young redheaded woman asked. "Who the hell is this?"

"Honey, Emma, this is Persephone, the goddess—"

"The Goddess of Spring," she finished for him. "Awesome. Why is she here instead of the Underworld? It's November! And does she know she's pregnant?"

"Of course I know," Persephone huffed. That human woman probably thought she was daft.

"Well, you can't be too sure," Emma replied, "I mean you *are* here and it's the end of fall. Is your curse broken?"

Oh, how she wished. "I'm afraid not. Who are you?"

"I'm sorry," Ares said. "Emma, this is Persephone."

"You said that already."

"And Persephone, this is my wife, Emma."

Well, that was interesting. The God of War had wed a human woman. "It is nice to meet you, but I have to be on my way now. She turned toward the door.

"No can do." Ares stood in her path with his arms crossed over his large chest. "Not until we figure out what's going on."

Persephone had always known Ares as a short fused, angry man, but this god who stood in front of her was different. Everything about him was different from the way he stood, the way he talked, and especially the way he looked at Emma. Where the Ares she'd known had been overbearing and impatient, this man was calm and cautious. What could have changed him so profoundly?

"It's okay," Emma told her. "Come with me. I want to show you something."

"I really cannot stay," Persephone argued as Emma took her by the elbow.

"This won't take long, and if you still want to leave, we'll let you go," Emma promised.

Persephone went with her, through the house and down a hallway to a white door. Emma opened it quietly and went inside. A soft light lit one corner of the room, giving just enough light to see by. She walked over to a crib.

"This is Rhya," Emma told her.

Persephone did not remember following Emma into the room, but she found herself standing over the crib, gazing down at the sleeping infant. "The Goddess of Fertility?"

"That's her namesake," Emma told her.

"Is she Ares's child?"

Emma nodded. "And mine."

"She is beautiful," Persephone breathed. She couldn't help but wonder if her own child would hold such beauty. Without thinking, she reached for the little one and brushed a stray, red curl from her face.

"The reason I wanted you to meet her is because this little girl is everything to us. Ares wouldn't have brought you here if he planned to do anything but protect you. He would never put Rhya in harm's way."

Such a beautiful little life, Persephone thought. No wonder the God of War had calmed. He'd found true love and began a family. "Is his curse broken?"

Emma smiled. "It is."

The baby's eyes fluttered open, and Persephone couldn't help but stare into them. They were the bluest blue of a clear afternoon sky. The baby stared back at her with the wisdom of a thousand years, and as if she already knew her.

"Hi, baby girl," Emma cooed at the little one. "You're awake. Look who's come to visit."

When Emma looked at Persephone expectantly, she said, "Hello, Rhya, I'm Persephone."

The baby cooed at her, and she thought her heart might just explode from the sudden influx of love and adoration. She subconsciously clutched her chest to keep it all in.

"Would you like to hold her?" Emma asked.

She didn't wait for an answer, but rather picked up the child and placed her in Persephone's arms. The little one didn't weigh much at all, so precious and so tiny. She smelled of baby powder and lotion, flowers and, well, joy. Before that moment, Persephone had never smelled joy, but that was the emotion the scent of the baby invoked. She reached her little hand up and instinctively, the goddess leaned her face down. The soft, smooth skin of the baby's hand touched Persephone's cheek, and something inside of her broke. Tears flowed freely from her eyes, even as she smiled at the tiny baby.

"I'm sorry," she said, "I don't know why I'm crying."

"I do," Emma answered. "I want to promise you that everything will be okay, that nothing will go wrong, but I can't. I can, however, promise you that we, Ares and myself, along with a few close friends, will protect you. We will do everything in our power to see that you and your baby are safe and together."

"It is not possible," Persephone told her. "To be born under the curse is a fate worse than death."

"Then I guess we better start looking for a way to break your curse," Emma told her, taking the baby from her arms.

"I fear I don't have much longer," Persephone whispered. "I can't abandon my responsibilities, but I will die before my child suffers a curse that is not his own." This was the first time she had thought of her young as he instead of her. Now Persephone felt uncertain if she would give birth to a boy or a girl. *It doesn't matter*, she told herself, *as long as the baby is healthy.*

"I'm glad you feel that way," Emma said. "So would I."

"Well?" Ares came into the room and took Rhya into his arms. "Are you women conspiring against Daddy?" he asked the baby in a sing-song voice. "What are they trying to talk my little ginger snap into this time?"

Emma glared. "Stop calling her that."

"What? She likes it," he teased. "Don't you, baby girl? You're a daddy's girl."

Emma dropped her face into her palm and sighed. "This is what you have to look forward to."

"No, I don't," Persephone said with deep sadness. "But someone will."

"I told you, we are going to keep you and your baby together."

"Hold up," Ares said, tucking the baby into his arm. "We're doing *what*?"

"We're protecting them," Emma told him. "And helping her break her curse."

Ares backed up and shook his head. "Oh, hell no," he argued. "No way in *fuck* am I gonna stand between Hades and his wife! The *freaking* God of the Underworld? You've lost your mind. No. I won't do it."

"But you will," Emma told him definitively.

"No."

Chapter Five

Hades decided that for now, it was best to remain invisible. He closed his eyes and shut out all of the noise from the street and searched again for Olympian power. He could feel it beckoning him to the east, stronger than the power he'd felt from Apollo and Aphrodite. He could not afford to waste another minute. He ghosted himself to the location of that power. Cold water washed over his feet as soon as he materialized.

Hades jumped out of the water, the memory of his connection with the River Styx all too fresh in his mind. Looking around, he calmed himself immediately. He was not in the Underworld on the banks of the sorrowful river, but on the shore of the Atlantic Ocean. His feet sank into the soft, wet sand as the waters lapped playfully at the coast. Just across the sand was an elaborate beach house, sitting high above the land. It had been raised to accommodate the rising tides and surges of the water during storms. Nevertheless, it was fitting of a god. The opulent décor on the deck alone was a giveaway. The outer walls were painted to reflect the sun like gold, while crystal windchimes hung from the patio. The power within that abode was much stronger than that of his wife. This was power that rivaled his own.

"Zeus!" Hades shouted toward the house. "Get your ass out here, Brother!"

"Hades," Zeus said cheerfully, coming out onto his patio. "It's been a long time."

"Where is Persephone?"

"Hold on a minute; let me come down," Zeus told him, disappearing back into the house. A moment later, he and Hera walked out onto the sand.

"Why didn't you just ghost down here?" Hades asked.

Zeus's brows touched his hairline. "And use our powers? No, thank you."

"You're still afraid of that silly curse." Hades shook his head. "Yet here you are, free from Olympus."

"And the longer we are away from the sky mountain, the weaker we become," Hera told him. "That part of the curse is true."

There was no stopping his eyes from rolling. After he found Persephone, Hades was going to show these gods and goddesses what being an Olympian really meant. "I am searching for Persephone," he said. "I'm told Ares may know where to find her."

"Then why have you come to us instead of the God of War?" Hera asked.

"I don't know where New York is," Hades admitted. "I've searched for Persephone's power, but it is all but lost to me."

"Perhaps she has shielded herself from you," Zeus offered. "Maybe she's done being your prisoner."

"She is not my prisoner," Hades growled.

"Zeus," Hera said, placing her hand on his forearm, "stop that. Hades, your brother, has come to us for help. I think we should do it."

"Why would I help him?" Zeus snorted, then turned to ask Hades, "How the hell did you get out of the Underworld?"

"I escaped, but that's none of your concern. I need to find my wife. Where is she?"

"How the hell would I know?"

"Maybe we should help." Hera tightened her grip on Zeus's arm.

"Fuck that. Why would we help him? He's never been anything but a thorn in our side."

Hades's hair blazed as he growled at the god.

"Oh, that's scary. Are you done?" Zeus mocked him. "All you've done is cause trouble on Mount Olympus. Find your own damn wife. It's about time she left your sorry ass."

"Zeus, I think you're being a little harsh. It's not like she can just leave. Maybe there is something wrong?" Hera said gently.

Zeus glared at Hades, his face turning beet-red. "It's not our problem."

"It's the right thing to do," Hera said. "I can help get you to New York. You're almost there. Go north and stick to the East Coast. You'll find Ares near Central Park."

"Thank you, goddess," Hades said sincerely. "Zeus, I hope you enjoy your time on this beach and I also hope you choke on your own wine."

Hades nodded and ghosted himself away. He didn't know why Hera wanted to help him, but he was grateful for it. He didn't want to admit the relief he felt. Even though he would never admit it, not even to himself, he could feel his power slowly draining from his body. He had to find her and take her home sooner rather than later.

***

Persephone watched as Emma used her phone to call someone named Sharalyn. "Great, so I'll see you in—" she said into it, and then the woman was standing in the living room. She was of average height for a human, but this woman was no ordinary human. She had ghosted in without a thought to the use of her powers. She wasn't one of the gods, but she was definitely something.

"Hey," Sharalyn said to her. "You must be Persephone. So glad to meet you." She held out one hand covered in a sleek black glove. She was wearing tight black jeans and a fitted black shirt. It went well with her dark hair and blue eyes.

The Goddess of Spring took her hand and shook it. "I am. Who are you?"

The woman sat down on the sofa next to her and crossed her legs. "I'm Sharalyn, Thanatos' wife."

"You are not human," Persephone pointed out.

"Not exactly." She laughed. "I used to be before Thanatos tried to kill me. As it turns out, I don't play by the rules very well. Now I'm a reaper."

"I think we should just start at the beginning," Emma said, handing a cup of hot tea to Persephone and sitting down in the recliner. She crossed her ankles underneath her bottom and got comfortable. "You see, Poseidon was the first to break his curse."

"I heard about that," Persephone said. The God of the Sea had been willing to give up his own life to protect the mermaid he loved, and in doing so, he broke his curse.

"Yes, well, you see, my husband wasn't one to be outdone. When we met, I wanted to *pummel* him. He was rude, self-centered, egotistical, and just so *damned* irritating."

"Sounds right." Persephone laughed.

"But I learned to love him, and he loved me. He was willing to give up everything, including his freedom to protect me from Athena, who was hell bent on keeping us apart."

"But Athena isn't so bad," Sharalyn said. "I like her."

"Well, I do, too…now." Emma snickered. "But don't tell her that."

"I was never fond of Athena," Persephone added.

"Thor changed her quite a bit," Emma told her.

"We're getting out of order here," Sharalyn said. "After Ares broke his curse, Thanatos met me. I was supposed to die in a car accident, but for whatever reason, when he touched me, I didn't die. He tried repeatedly. So did I. When I started taking on his powers as he lost them, it became pretty obvious that I was the key to his curse. Hades wanted him to trick me into taking his place in the Underworld, but Thanatos couldn't do it. Long story short, here I am."

"My husband can be quite difficult," Persephone agreed.

"Then Ares saw Loki hanging out around town," Emma told Persephone. "Loki made up some bullshit lie to Thor, and then he came looking for us. He and Athena hit it off, Loki's out of commission, and now her curse is broken."

"The answer is love," Persephone said sadly.

"Yes," Emma agreed. "But why are you sad? Love will be the key to your freedom."

"Then I'm afraid that I can never be free." She wrung her hands together, holding back tears. "I have so much love to give, but there is no love for me. I don't blame Hades, but I fear he is incapable of such emotions."

"Then maybe it is someone else's love? Or the love for your child? Or hell, the world."

Persephone felt her heart breaking. She didn't want the love of someone else. She wanted Hades to love her as she loved him.

"But you don't want that," Sharalyn said as if she could read her mind. "You're in love with Hades."

"Is it that obvious?" she asked, hating herself for caring so much about someone who could never return it.

"As plain as the nose on your face," Emma said.

"Then I guess we'll just have to make him see how much you really mean to him," Sharalyn said.

"How can we do that?"

Emma patted her on the knee. "Don't you worry about that. You just leave it to us and do what we say."

"Yes." Sharalyn grinned. "Trust us."

"But Hades will come for me," she reminded them. "He will find me eventually."

"Probably," Emma said. "And I hope he does. But we aren't going to make it easy for him. We have friends in high places." She tapped on her phone for a moment and then set it on the table. It lit up, and Emma looked at it and smiled. "And those friends are on their way to us."

Chapter Six

Within minutes, there was a knock on the door. Ares opened it, and none other than the God of Thunder walked through. "Hey, Pixie," he rumbled teasingly, swinging his hammer, Mjölnir, carelessly at his side. His attire was fitting to the modern human world, but anyone with eyes could plainly see that he was anything but human. His hair was trimmed close to his skull, showing the ancient runes that were tattooed onto the skin of his neck. The runes traveled down his arms, past the short sleeves of his black T-shirt. His enormous body was crammed into a pair of jeans and heavy boots on his feet.

"Fuck off, pansy." Ares smiled at him.

Persephone smiled, as well. The two had been enemies for so long, it was nice to see them getting along in their manly-man kind of way.

"Move aside," a familiar female voice said. Athena pushed between the men and made a beeline for the infant swing where the baby was swaying quietly. She picked up Rhya and snuggled her close to her chest.

Athena appeared quite different from the last time Persephone had seen her. Her battle gear was no more, as was her robes and jewels. It was as if she'd given up all indicators of her station on Olympus. The biggest difference, though, was the smile on her face. Athena had always been beautiful, with her flowing blonde hair, brilliant cobalt-blue eyes, and the body of a Valkyrie, but there had always been a sadness within her, an unrest that she could never fully hide. However, holding little Rhya, that sadness melted away, and she glowed from the inside out with true happiness.

"Hello, Athena," Persephone said softly.

The Goddess of Wisdom and Strategy turned and graced Persephone with a brilliant smile. "Are you ready for one of these?"

Pushing the sadness deep down inside, Persephone forced another smile. "It has been a wonderful journey," she said. "But I fear what is to come."

"Don't be silly," Athena told her. "You're the goddess of spring. You got this."

"I'm not scared of motherhood. I'm afraid that I will not be his mother."

"Well, why wouldn't you be?"

"I cannot stay in this realm," Persephone reminded her. "I must return to the Underworld." She recapped her reasons as to why she didn't want her child born under the weight of the curse.

"Well, break the curse," Athena said as if it were as easy as breathing.

"That's what I said," Sharalyn told her. "She's in love with Hades."

"Fuck our lives," Athena grumbled, putting the baby back into her swing. "Couldn't you fall in love with someone else? Apollo is cute."

"Seriously, Athena?" Emma asked. "You know the heart wants what it wants."

Athena nodded. "I do. Very well." Her eyes lifted to her husband who was talking with Ares. They were speaking softly, no doubt about all that had transpired. "Why can't we just catch a break?"

"That would be awesome, but no."

"Persephone *has* a break." Thor interrupted. "She has something that others do not. She has us. I, Thor, the God of Thunder, have vowed to protect her and her unborn child. I will crush Hades and free her of this wretched curse."

"There will be no crushing," Athena said.

"But if we smite Hades," Ares jumped in, "Persephone won't have to worry about him and his damned curse."

"Hades deserves to be free as well," Persephone said softly.

"Hades is a dick," Ares retorted. "I don't plan on going on to the Underworld before my time."

"Valhalla is a wondrous place, the resting place for all eternity for true warriors," Thor said. "I'm not ready to go, either. Therefore, we must strike before Hades finds her. We must put him down like the dog he is."

"There will be no attacking and there will be no smiting," Emma said definitively. "Hades is the key to breaking her curse."

"Exactly. It's his damned fault she's cursed to the Underworld," Ares said.

"He will bask in the bitter taste of defeat when I shove Mjölnir down his throat, ripping his spine from his body." Thor flipped the hammer as if it weighed nothing.

"You don't understand." Athena tried to explain.

"Death to the Lord of the Underworld!" Ares cried.

"Prepare to meet your end!" Thor shouted toward the heavens.

"Stop!" Persephone yelled at them. "Just stop."

"I thought you wanted our help?" Thor asked, clearly confused.

"I was happy on my own until you came along and kidnapped me," Persephone said, pointing at Ares and doing her best to hold back the tears that threatened her eyes. All of that talk of hurting Hades had made her insides crumble and her throat burn. No, she could not allow it. "I will not allow you to smite, crush, or end Hades."

"I know that you're all about life," Ares said, "but what are we supposed to do?"

"I don't know," Persephone said. "I don't. I just want to go."

"Guys," Emma stood up and faced them, "She's in love with him."

Ares and Thor looked at each other with equal expressions of shock. Thor ran his hand over his skull-trimmed hair and shook his head. Ares's mouth opened and closed several times, but no sound escaped him. After a minute, Ares growled. "What in the—fuck my life. I need a drink."

"I'm with you, Brother," Thor agreed, and the two stomped off toward the kitchen.

Persephone watched them leave the room, forcing her breathing under control. "I know that Hades is not the easiest person to like, but I can't condone hurting him."

"They're men," Athena said, dropping herself onto the sofa and crossing her legs. "They don't know any better."

"Gender is no excuse for bad manners," a disembodied voice said.

Persephone's heart jumped into her chest and she visually searched the room. "Who's there?" she demanded.

"I apologize," the woman's voice said again. She slowly became visible next to the large front window. "Sometimes I forget that you can't see me."

The woman was tall and slender, with inky-black hair that was braided down her back. Her golden robes flowed around her as if a breeze had spun around her body. "Hello, Freya," Persephone said cautiously. "What are you doing here?"

"I've come to lend my power," the Norse goddess said with a smile.

"Why?" Persephone knew there was never any love loss between the Olympians and the Asgardians. It made no sense for Freya to come to this realm.

"It wasn't too long ago that I was in need of help, even if I didn't know it, and these fine people risked everything to show me the error of my ways. They helped me to find my true power, and to banish Loki back to his prison rock. This time for good."

"We thought Loki was dead," Emma said. "How did he ever survive that?"

"An immortal is extremely difficult to kill," Freya reminded them. "I used a spell to bind him with Fenrir's entrails. The blood bond is impossible to break."

"That's disgusting." Emma scrunched her face in distaste.

"It really is," Sharalyn agreed. "So, Freya, did Emma already fill you in?"

The goddess nodded. "She did. I have come bearing gifts." She reached into her robes and pulled out a small wooden box. "This is for you, Goddess of Spring." When she held it out, Persephone took it from her.

"What is it?" she asked, admiring the beautiful runes that were carved into the planes of the Birchwood.

"It's a spell," Freya told her. "Open it."

Did she really want to open that box? Why not, though? It was just a box. *So was Pandora's Box,* a little voice in her mind said. *It's not about the box, but what's inside.*

"It's okay." Emma patted her on the arm reassuringly. "Freya is good people. We are all here to help."

Persephone nodded. What choice did she have? None. She knew that she was taking a risk and it was a selfish one. Keeping herself on Earth and wasting her power was the most selfish thing she'd ever done. She deserved the curse on her shoulders. With a flip of her finger, the box was open. A beautiful ring was inside. The band was golden, lined with green leaves that wound around the gold.

"It's gorgeous," she breathed.

"It will protect you from your curse," Freya told her. "I know that Demeter spelled you to hide you, but I can see even that is waning. You need some serious protection."

"I thought she might have come to me," Persephone said quietly as she slipped the ring on her middle finger, "But she has not."

"Of course not," Emma said. "I wouldn't. If anyone from Olympus is looking for you, Demeter is the first place they're gonna check. It would kill me, but I would stay away from Rhya to protect her."

Persephone inclined her head. She understood, but still, it hurt. She needed her mother. A pair of frail, human arms wrapped around her shoulders. Emma. Then another pair of arms. And another. All of the women had sensed her sadness and were holding her, and it felt good. The tears flowed freely from her eyes as she let herself sink into the unconditional love and support these incredible women provided her. She felt her body warm from the inside out under the weight of their arms. Someone laid her head on Persephone's back. She hadn't realized that she'd been cold before. Perhaps it wasn't her mother, specifically, that she had needed, but the support of someone who would stand by her. As their faith seeped into her pores, Persephone began to believe that these women could and would help her. They would protect her, and by extension, their husbands would as well. For the first time since her journey had begun, the Goddess of Spring was beginning to see a light at the end of the tunnel. She began to believe she could do this.

"We will protect you," Sharalyn said.

"I know," Persephone told her, lifting her head and straightening her spine. The ladies moved away from her, allowing her to stand on her own again. "Thank you, Freya." She gazed at the ring on her finger.

"As long as you wear it," Freya told her, "You will be protected from the curse. Sleep in it. Bathe in it. Never take it off."

There were no words to describe how much appreciation Persephone felt at that moment. "I will return your kindness one day."

"Nonsense. Now, I'm going back to Asgard to watch for that husband of yours. Someone needs to ensure that he does not get into any trouble that he can't get out of." She looked up and a rainbow of color surrounded her as the Bifrost lifted her away back to her home on Asgard.

Chapter Seven

As soon as Hades focused to the north, he felt a surge of power. It was definitely immortal power, and not the kind that was hindered by the curse. It had to be Ares. It was power that reminded him of the old days when the gods roamed freely. It was so powerful that Hades couldn't pinpoint its exact location. It seemed to be spread out across a large area. He ghosted to the epicenter of the power in hopes that he'd land right in Ares's face.

He materialized on something metal, high in the sky. "What the hell?" Hades cursed. He was atop a statue in the middle of a body of water. "Where have I landed now?" He looked at the tall buildings and the lights of the city nearby. This place pulsed with power, as if more than one god were present. It made it nearly impossible to decipher whose power it was.

Unwilling to admit that he'd missed his mark, Hades ghosted to the top of a building across the bay. Once he landed, he searched the streets for any clue as to where to go next. He watched as humans milled by, carrying on with their short lives as if the Goddess of Spring wasn't missing, and the entire world weren't at risk. They laughed with each other as if there weren't a care in the world. They cared for nothing but themselves, and yet, it was the Olympians that bore the curse, not these humans that the Creator cared so much for. He wondered if they would care when their world froze over.

Two men walking side by side caught his attention and interrupted his inner bitching. They were far enough away that he could not see their faces, but something about the way they carried themselves was familiar. Pulling Aphrodite's cape tighter around him, he ghosted closer to them.

Ares! And was that—*Thor*? Why in all of the Underworld were those two walking together as if they were the best of friends? They must have conspired to kidnap Persephone and hold her hostage! Rage boiled in his veins, but Hades knew that an explosive display of his power was not going to help find his wife. If he smote these two buffoons, they would be unable to lead him to his wife. No, he would follow them instead.

Keeping himself invisible and far enough away to avoid detection, he followed them. The pair chuckled like fools as they maneuvered the busy streets. Hades couldn't help but wonder what was so damned funny, so he closed some of the distance between himself and Ares.

"Fear me, I am the Lord of the Underworld," Ares mocked. "Look at my flaming hair."

"I shall put out his fire!" Thor guffawed.

"He's a ginger in every sense of the word," Ares said. "Right down to the stealing of souls. He has never cared about anything but himself. I don't know why the women think he could be free. If anyone deserves that curse, it's Hades."

Shoving the growl back down his throat, Hades kept pace with them. Just as soon as

Persephone was safely back at home, these two would taste Hades's fire. He would condemn them both to the fiery pits of Tartarus.

They left the inner city, and soon, the building became residential. They were in the suburbs. Hades watched as Ares and Thor walked right up to one and entered the front door. This had to be Ares's domicile.

Hades kept himself invisible as he crept around the perimeter of the building. A sound he'd thought he may not hear again had him looking through an open window. She was there. Persephone was talking to a human woman, and whatever the woman said made her laugh. Without thinking, Hades ran to the house at full speed, intending to crash through that window and rescue his wife.

Just before he would have shattered the glass, an invisible force slammed him backward. He landed on his ass in the dirt, sliding out of control. "What the hell is this cursed place? There is magic here. What has the God of War done?" he thought aloud.

There was only one explanation, and it was witchcraft.

Hades stomped around to the front door. If he couldn't crash through a window, perhaps he would just use the door that the God of War himself had gone through. His feet landed heavily on the wooden steps as he marched to the flimsy wood door. He wrapped his hand around the knob and turned it.

Electric fire shot up his arm, radiating over his chest and spreading throughout his body. There was no stopping the roar of pain from escaping his throat. "Ares!" he bellowed. "Open this godforsaken door!"

When no one rushed to allow him entrance, Hades kicked the door. As he picked himself up from the lawn a second time, he cursed himself for thinking it would work and glanced around to make sure no one had seen him bounce back, as if he'd been shot from a rubber band. He clomped back up the stairs and stood in front of the door. He forced himself to breathe in and out, evening out his temper until he could be calm. He pulled the cape off his shoulders and his Helm of Darkness from his head, tucking it neatly under his arm. Then, he knocked politely on the wooden door.

***

In addition to the women, Thanatos and Poseidon had arrived to assist in any way they could. The men had been discussing strategies while the women were making plans to care for the baby. Emma and Sharalyn had ordered so many baby supplies off the internet that Persephone didn't know where she would put it all. She was grateful for their help, no matter the form it came in. Her child would need supplies, far more than the ones she had already procured.

Ares did not seem surprised when there was a knock at the front door. Persephone watched as he calmly opened it to see a furious Hades on the other side.

His hair was disheveled, as if he'd spent an inordinate amount of time running his hand through it. His eyes were surrounded by dark circles and he appeared haggard, as if he'd had a very long few days. Her heart went out to him and she had to resist the urge to go to him, to make his worries go away.

"Give me my wife back," he snarled at Ares.

Ares shook his head. "No can do."

Hades tried to push his way into the house, but the protection spell would not allow it. "What sorcery is this?" he demanded. "You have no right to keep me from her!"

"Whoa, my Underworld-dwelling little brother, slow your roll," Poseidon said, holding out his hand in a stop motion.

Hades glared at him. "Having the same father does not make us brothers," he hissed at Poseidon.

"Actually, it kind of does," Poseidon told him.

"Has he hit his head?" Thor asked. "The man is daft!"

"Why is that hammer-wielding sissy here?" Hades demanded.

"I am no sissy," Thor bristled, "and you would benefit from remembering that."

"Shut the fuck up, or you'll be picking your own teeth from your colon," Hades growled at him, then he turned back to Poseidon. "And you! If you were a real brother, you would help me and *give back my wife*! I *will* have my wife back and I shall crush those who would stand in my way. Make no mistake. *I am* the Lord of the Underworld, and I will reign in the blood of my enemies."

Just as she became certain that everything was going to fall apart, Poseidon pushed his way outside and closed the door behind him.

***

"Look," Poseidon said to Hades, "I understand. I was without the woman I loved once, too."

"This is not about love." Hades snorted. "It's about you taking what's mine."

Poseidon pursed his lips and nodded. "Okay, okay. But let's just say for the sake of argument that you are genuinely worried about her." When Hades only raised a brow at him, he continued, "Persephone is safe here. There is enough magic in and around this house to protect her from you, the curse, and anyone else who would do her harm."

"Then let me in," Hades growled through gritted teeth.

"No. Because you can't go in until you're invited, and there is no way you're getting an invite until you calm the fuck down."

"I'm not a fucking vampire."

"No, and you are far from reasonable right now."

"I am calm," Hades muttered under his breath.

"Yeah, and I'm a fairy." Poseidon chuckled. "Look, put your hair out. Stop using your power all willy-nilly or you won't have any left."

"That's bullshit," he said. "I have plenty of power and I am ready to use it to tear this house and its magic down!"

Poseidon shrugged. "Okay then. Let's go." He took Hades by the shoulder and ghosted them to the swamps of New Orleans.

"What the hell?"

"Listen, Brother," Poseidon said. "Whether you believe it or not, I *am* helping you. I'm sorry that it has to be the hard way, but whatever works, right? What do you say? The end justifies the means? Well, this is the means, and I hope you come to your senses so that the end is a happy one." Then, Poseidon ghosted away, leaving Hades standing in the muddy waters of the swamp.

Chapter Eight

"Have you lost your ever-loving mind?" Zeus demanded of Hera. "Why did you help him? He doesn't deserve our help!"

Hera tilted her head, her blonde curls tumbling over her shoulder, and smiled. "Of course he doesn't," she agreed. "But you know how this works. If Persephone doesn't take her ass back to the Underworld, she can't recharge her power. If she becomes human, we might as well go ahead and return to Olympus, because I'm not living through another ice age."

"She might go back in time," he said. "She's very responsible."

"She *will* be returning." Hera turned and conjured a suitcase. "I'm going to ensure that our little home stays nice and toasty all summer." She began filling the suitcase with clothes. "You coming?"

Zeus shook his head. "I want no part of this. We raised our children and now they must fend for themselves."

Hera spun around and glared at him. "You did none of the raising," she growled. "You were too busy dipping your pen in any inkwell that came along. You donated your seed while leaving behind a string of single mothers who did what they could to raise their children alone. You claim to be the king, the head of the family, but you know nothing of family. You took me as your wife, because at the time, there was a serious lack of options. Then you proceeded to use me as your personal baby factory, as your maid, until we made others. I was nothing but a tool to you, and neither were your children. You are Zeus, the God of Lightning, King; you are powerful, quick to smite, a despicable man-whore, but don't you dare call yourself a father." She slammed her suitcase closed and picked it up in her hand. "I'll be taking the Porsche. Don't follow me."

Zeus watched her storm out of the beach house in a huff. His mouth hung open, unable to find the words to say to her. As the Porsche peeled out of the garage, he ran his hand over his dark hair. "I can't believe she just talked to me that way."

***

Where the hell was he? Why had Poseidon brought him to this place? And what the hell was that smell? Hades looked to his left and then to his right, then to the place where the God of the Sea had just stood moments before. The sun was setting to the west and all he could see was mud, water, and trees. He was in a godforsaken swamp. The water lapped at his calves and something brushed his skin. "Fuck!" he growled as he trudged his way to the edge of the water. It smelled. Horribly. It was like standing in a heavily used toilet. He was going to give his brother a piece of his mind, and he was doing it right now.

Hades focused his mind on New York and ghosted. When he materialized, he was still in the swamp. Two feet from him was an enormous alligator, its mouth open and ready to strike. His heart leapt in his chest, thundering out of control. He quickly ghosted again, landing at yet another location within the swampland. He closed his eyes and concentrated. Ghosting again, he found himself at the edge of the swamp. When he turned, he could still see the last spot in which he'd stood.

"Fucking Poseidon," he grumbled. He didn't know what the god had done to his powers, but they were getting weaker. He stomped off toward the city lights that he could see ahead. "Put your hair out," he mocked. "Fuck you, brother."

Something pinched in his sandal and Hades looked down. There was a tiny lobster between his toes! He shook his foot, but the little bugger wouldn't let go. Stinging pain lanced up his leg, and Hades snatched the little thing off his foot, tearing the skin. "Son of a bitch!" he cursed. "What the hell is that thing? A tiny bringer of pain and death?" He slung the monster behind him into the muddy waters. "I'm gonna kill that overgrown fish when I get back," he grumbled. Or perhaps it would be better fitting to call Poseidon a snake. A devious snake that was hell-bent on making Hades's life hell. Well, he had another thing coming. Hell was what Hades did, and he was going to unleash it on his too-pretty brother. He was gonna smash his teeth and see what the women thought of him then.

Hades walked until his feet were screaming at him in pain. Why the hell was he feeling pain? He entered the city and headed for the well-lit section that had people filling the streets. It was well past dark by this point, and he wondered what they were all doing out so late. As he turned onto a street, the sign said, "Bourbon Street." He knew this was a street of merriment and drinking. An all-night party for humans. Good. He would get refreshments and a change of clothes. He smelled like a pig.

There was an establishment serving beverages that had a long line in front of it. Hades didn't care for the line; he was thirsty and offending humans was the last thing he cared about. He pushed past the line of patrons to the counter. "I require mead," he told the young man behind the counter.

"I got hurricanes," he said.

"I want mead," Hades growled.

"I have hurricanes," the man repeated as if Hades was daft.

"Look, you little—"

"I'll buy you a drink," a woman said. She was obviously a little tipsy, slurring her words. "One hurricane for the hottie!" She placed several dollars on the counter and the man handed Hades a tall, curved glass.

As he took the beverage, he realized it was not glass, but made of plastic. It was white with a little umbrella sticking out at the top. Hades poured it into his mouth, enjoying the cold concoction. It was sweet and tangy at the same time. He downed the whole cup and set the plastic back on the counter. "Thank you," he said. As he turned to leave, what felt like a knife jabbed through the roof of his mouth and into his brain. Hades's hands flew to his head, pressing on either side as if it would stop his brain from exploding.

"Brain freeze." The man laughed. "Gotta go slower."

Hades turned away, his hands still on his head and fled the establishment. What the hell had he walked into? This place was full of sorcery and spells—he could feel it all around him. He needed to get the hell out of Dodge before some witch put a spell on him. The pain in his head finally subsided as he traversed the busy street. He noticed that people all dressed far differently than he did. Some were wearing simple, peasant attire, while others wore fighting gear, like the two women he saw walking in front of him. One was taller than the other with long, black hair the color of charcoal. The other had brown hair that hung down her back. It did nothing to conceal the jeweled sword that was secured between her shoulder blades. They walked with confidence, as if they were on a mission. The black-haired one turned around and glared at him. Hades stopped in his tracks when he saw her brilliant green eyes. The brunette followed suit, staring him down as if she were trying to decide if he were a threat. Valkyries?

Amazons? When the black-haired woman produced yellow-colored light in her hand, Hades knew. Witches.

He prepared to fight them, taking his battle stance, but the brunette placed her hand on the other's arm. "He's not here for us," she said. "Come on, Sis." The pair turned to leave him, no longer interested in his presence.

Hades wondered why they had turned to him in the first place. It didn't matter, he decided. He had more important things to do, like beat the snot out of Poseidon and Ares, and then return his wife to the Underworld.

He found a shop that sold attire. Standing in front of it was a slender man wearing a deep purple suit and shoes that were polished to a high shine. Women surrounded him, touching his chest and arms, hanging on his every word. That's what he needed. He needed attire fitting this world and something that would command respect. Hades went past the man and entered the store.

Clothing in all sizes hung on racks. He found a rack that had colorful suits like the man out front had been wearing. It took some searching, but he was able to find one that would fit his enormous frame. It was the color of rubies and the material was soft, like crushed velvet.

Kicking off his sandals, Hades pulled the pants on his legs. He was very aware of the stares he was getting, but he did not care. He needed fresh clothes. The trousers were a little snug and he had a hard time getting his manly jewels in them comfortably. It took several tries to get the tiny button fastened, but he finally got it. He wiggled his hips within the snug material a few times to get them just right. Then he pulled his armor over his head. It dropped to the floor with a loud thud. He slipped his arms into the suit jacket, which was lined with soft material like silk. It barely buttoned around his torso, leaving his manly chest hair exposed. *Yes,* he thought as he smoothed his hands down the front of his suit, *this was just what he needed.*

Picking up his gear, he tucked the Helm of Darkness under his arm and wrapped his armor in Aphrodite's cloak, then proceeded to the man behind the counter. "You there," he commanded, pointing at the man, "I will require a satchel for my armor."

The man raised a brow at Hades. "A what?"

God save him from insolent idiots. "A satchel. A bag," he said with a roll of his eyes. He didn't want to smite the man, but he wasn't above it.

The man slowly pulled a large plastic bag out from under the counter and held it out for Hades. "Let me just ring you up," he said.

Hades huffed at him as he shoved his armor into the plastic bag. As he was headed toward the door, he heard the man say, "You have to pay for that stuff."

Spinning around, Hades pinned the man with a glare. "I am the Lord of the Underworld. I don't pay for shit." Then he walked out the door. He heard the man behind him saying, "It's okay, it was on clearance anyway."

After leaving Bourbon Street, it became clear that it was going to take far longer than he realized to get back to New York. He'd grabbed a map from a street vendor and looked at his location. It would take him days to walk to New York. He needed a chariot. He would've ghosted there if he could, but damn his brother for pointing out that his powers were waning. He saw just the one he wanted only a block away.

It was sleek, black, and had large wheels for moving quickly. The hood had a vent for the horses underneath as well. The man sitting in it was talking on a device like the one Aphrodite had. Hades knocked on the window.

When the man opened the window a tiny bit, Hades said, "I require the use of your chariot."

The man inside chuckled and rolled the window back up. Anger rose up in his chest as Hades knocked again. This time the man inside ignored him. How *dare* he ignore the Lord of the Underworld? Grinding his teeth in frustration, Hades yanked on the door handle and opened it. The man was caught by surprise as Hades grabbed him by the shirt and pulled him out, tossing him onto the street like a ragdoll.

"Hey!" the man shouted as he stood up. "That's my Mustang!"

Hades got in and slammed the door closed. He pushed the button that locked the car. Now, how to get it going… "Heyaah," he said to the horses. Nothing happened. "Go!" Nothing. "Start!"

The engine roared to life and Hades smiled. The owner was knocking on the window, but Hades ignored him. Now, to go. There was a wheel for steering, and a lot of buttons. There was a rod in the middle that Hades didn't know what it was for. There were three pedals on the floor, and he mashed one down with his foot. The engine roared and the car jerked but went nowhere.

"Come on, man! You don't even know how to drive a stick!" the man at the window was shouting.

Hades shoved the rod forward and the chariot jerked again. He mashed the pedal and the metal transport moved a few feet, jolted, made a horrendous noise, then stopped. The chariot was quiet. "Start!" Hades shouted at it. It came back to life. This time, Hades tried to remember what he'd done to make it move the first time. He pushed in the two pedals on the left, pushed the rod forward again, then he pushed the pedal on the far right. The transport roared but did not move. "Oh, right," he said as he lifted his foot from the far-left pedal. A ridiculous grinding noise vibrated the whole chariot and then it moved. Hades kept his foot on the pedal as he slowly pulled out onto the road. The man was still hitting the chariot, but Hades was in motion. The engine made some odd noises, but at least it was moving.

The man lost contact with his vehicle and dropped to his knees on the street.

Hades opened the window to stick out his hand and wave at him.

"You're stripping the gears!" the man cried as Hades left him behind.

Chapter Nine

Persephone leaned against the doorframe and watched as Emma laid her infant down in her crib. Subconsciously, her hands went to her swollen belly. Her heart swelled with the love she already felt for the tiny baby growing inside of her.

"She is precious," she whispered.

Emma smiled and nodded. "Yes, she is. I think she's gonna be a handful when she's older." The two women left the room, Emma closing the door softly behind her. "Yours will be, too."

Persephone looked down at her belly. "I hope so. I hope that I am there to see it."

"You will be," Emma promised. When she would have walked away, Persephone took her wrist in hand.

"Promise me," Persephone begged. "Promise me that you will care for him if I cannot."

"Persephone," Emma breathed, taking both of the goddess's hands. "We're going to break that curse."

"Promise me."

"I promise," Emma said.

"Promise me that you, not some stranger, but you will love him if I cannot stay." She could feel the tears threatening to brim over, but she forced them back. Her baby needed her to be strong. "I don't want someone who can't protect him. I don't want a stranger. I want you. You and Ares. I want to know that if we can't break the curse, that at least my child will have a happy, safe life here with you." She took a deep breath and let it out. "I see the way the God of War has changed. I see the way he holds his daughter. I can feel the love you share as a family. That's what I want for my child, and if things do not go the way we hope, I need to know that he'll have that."

Worry lined etched over Emma's face, and she worried her bottom lip in her teeth for a moment. "We must talk to Ares about this," she finally said.

Persephone nodded. It was logical to speak with Ares first. This was an enormous responsibility that she was asking of her new friend. She followed Emma back into the living room where Poseidon had returned. He was sitting in the recliner with his feet propped up on the ottoman.

"Sit," Emma told her. "Relax. I'll talk to Ares and get you something to eat. It's dinnertime anyway."

Persephone felt so much gratitude for Emma. How had she survived on her own without the guidance of this human woman? Without all of her new friends? She watched as Athena kissed Thor gently on his cheek, how Thanatos stroked Sharalyn's sleek hair, and how Ares loved his family. Breaking their curses had made them far more human than the curse ever had, and they all seemed better for it. Not only did they possess their powers, but they possessed them in a way that wasn't just for victory, but for the greater good. Even Poseidon had broken his curse, finding happiness with the mermaid he'd fallen for so many years ago. Yes, this was a good home for her child. He would be happy here.

"So," Ares said, coming into the room, "I hear you want me to be your baby's godfather?"

"What?" Poseidon asked, leaning forward in the chair. "I want to be a godfather!"

"I am the perfect godfather," Thor announced, his chest puffing out more than it already was. "I have many talents."

"Shut up, Sea God," Ares said.

"I want to ensure that my child has a safe, loving home if I am not able to stay with him," Persephone told them all. "Emma and Ares already have a young daughter."

"Exactly. Which is why he should live with us," Thanatos said. "We don't have any children. He would be spoiled rotten."

"Oh, that's nice," Poseidon huffed. "Let's just let the baby live with the God of Death! Because *that* won't give him any psychological issues."

They all argued over who would make the best surrogate parents, and all Persephone could do was watch.

"Shut it, you big lug!"

"You're no better!"

"Enough!" Persephone said, standing and holding out her hand. "That's enough. I wanted to ask Emma because she has shown me that there is hope for our kind. She took Ares in and loved him, just the way he is, and I know that she would love my child, too. I expect all of you to play a part in raising my child, whether I am able to stay or not." She looked at Sharalyn. "You will help him learn his strengths, because you had to find yours." Then at Thanatos. "You will teach him to be persistent." To Poseidon: "You will teach him to swim and to control his anger, lest he harm someone." To Thor: "You will teach him courage and strength." To Athena: "You will teach him to think before he acts." To Ares: "And you will teach him when to fight, and when to let it be." She addressed all of the gods and goddesses in the house. "You will all have a hand in his upbringing, and I shall not have it any other way. But if I cannot be here, Emma will be his mother in my stead."

Emma's hand laid over her own heart and she nodded. "Persephone, Goddess of Spring, I would consider it an honor to care for your child. I promise you, I will love him, I will keep him safe, and we will all look after him. I also promise that we will help you break your curse."

"What even is your curse?" Sharalyn asked.

Persephone sat back down. "I know it by heart," she said. "I read it so many times, but I just cannot see a way to break it."

"Tell us," Athena prompted. "It can't be worse than mine."

Persephone nodded. She recited the words that had haunted her for a millennium. "Bound to one cursed by fate, for a time an unwilling mate, the gift of life you shall give, uncursed, the new one will live. Bring forth the love he does not see, opening his heart shall set you free."

They all sat in silence for a moment. "At least yours rhymes," Athena said on a laugh.

"Oh, my gawd!" Sharalyn said, jumping to her feet. "You're already on the path! Your curse is about to be broken!"

"I don't understand," Persephone said, shaking her head.

"The *baby*. A new life uncursed, open Hades's heart! If your baby is born and Hades realizes how much he loves you, then *boom*. Curse broken."

"I agree," Athena said.

"What did you do with Hades, anyway?" Emma asked Poseidon.

"I dumped him in a swamp so he could cool off," the Sea God answered.

"What's Hades's curse?" Ares asked. "They're tied together, right?"

Persephone nodded. She knew Hades's curse as well as her own. "Bound in love, bound in hate, until the bonds dissolve in fate. A life to give more precious than your own, a decision that will change the status quo. A prisoner to the afterlife you'll always be, a selfless act shall set you free."

"Fucking "selfless act" shit again," Poseidon grumbled.

"What do you suppose it means?" Persephone asked. She'd had her own ideas, but if she was right, they were screwed.

"It means he has to be willing to give his own life for someone or something," Thanatos said. "I had to give mine for Sharalyn."

"Me too," Poseidon said. "Mine said, the dragon's fire will set you free. It was total bullshit. I had to jump in front of a dragon, who was breathing fire, to save my wife. That's how my curse broke."

"Ares was willing to give up his freedom, his own life for me," Emma said.

It was worse than she'd expected. "Well, in that case, we're screwed. Hades doesn't love anyone. Especially not anyone he'd give his life for."

"I don't know," Poseidon said. "He seemed pretty upset."

"Only because I defied him," Persephone explained.

"I don't think so," the Sea God continued. "He was all a mess about it. He may not realize it, but he loves you. Does he know you're pregnant?" When Persephone shook her head, he groaned. "No wonder. He needs to know."

"Absolutely not," Ares insisted. "No."

"That's the key," Sharalyn said. "A new life uncursed, a life more precious than any known… that's definitely it."

"We can tell him when he finds his way back to us," Thanatos said. "I wanna see this one."

"Where is he?"

"In the swamp in New Orleans," Poseidon told them again. "It might take him a while to get back. He's got very little power."

A ball of lead formed in Persephone's stomach. What if he used all of his power? He would be human. Then who would run the Underworld? "I pray that you know what you're doing," she said softly.

"No worries," Poseidon assured her. "I got this. Hey, can I get a beer or something?"

"Get out of my chair," Ares grumbled at him. "Don't you have an elaborate underwater palace to go to, Sea God?"

"Yeah," Poseidon said sheepishly, "About that."

"Oh, no," Emma muttered. "What now?"

"I might have been told to get out and to stop breathing her air," he answered.

"What did you do?" Sharalyn asked warily.

"I only suggested that she might be gaining a little weight, and that I could conjure us a gym if she wanted to get into shape."

"You *are* daft," Thor said, shaking his head.

"You did *what*?" Emma barked.

"Idiot." Sharalyn sighed.

"I'll get you a blanket," Ares offered. It looked like the Sea God was spending the night.

Chapter Ten

Yet another chariot thundered past him on the road, its horn blaring as it went by. "Surely this thing can go faster," Hades grumbled, pushing down harder on the pedal. The transport made a horrendous noise, then something popped loudly. "I only have two horses and they can go faster than this!" He passed through a residential area that had dwellings in every color of the rainbow. What had gotten into humans? Perhaps they'd gone colorblind in this area? It was probably from the smell of that wretched pig hole he'd climbed out of.

He'd only been on the road for about an hour, and it seemed that he would never get to his destination. He'd chosen the wrong chariot if he wanted to get there any kind of fast. And what was that smell? It smelled like burning rubber. Hades touched his hair to ensure that it wasn't him. Nope. Ahead he saw a sign that said, "Truck Stop." There were a lot of people stopping their vehicles.

He decided he would stop there as well. Perhaps his chariot needed a rest.

He carefully maneuvered into the lot, never once letting off on the pedal. He didn't dare stop again, knowing his vehicle would not start up another time. He didn't care how many people had to swerve to avoid him or how many horns blared. They could bow to his way or get off the road. As soon as he was off the road, Hades let off the pedal and the vehicle rolled to a stop. Black smoke was pouring out from under the vented hood and every light inside was flashing. He had no idea what "Check Engine" or "Check Oil" meant, let alone any of the other lights or beeps that he'd been subjected to.

He got out of the chariot, deciding that he must look under the hood. He yanked up on it, but it was stuck firm. Using his godlike strength, Hades ripped the hood off. Smoke filled his eyes and nose, causing him to cough. He waved the smoke away, only to see that there were flames dancing around the metal centerpiece. He did not, however, see any horses under there.

The flames grew, and Hades tried to wave them off. Someone grabbed him, pulling him away from his chariot. "Unhand me now, you insolent fool!" he shouted, yanking his arm away from the stranger. "How dare you put your hands on me!"

"Look, buddy, I was saving your ass," the man answered. He was nearly as tall as Hades, but not as broad in the shoulders. His hair was thinning, and he had a good-sized belly underneath his green jumper that he wore.

"I do not need saving!" Hades snorted. "I am—"

Boom!

Hades jerked his head back to the chariot that had blown up, now engulfed in flames. "Fuck."

"Yeah," the man said. "You're welcome."

"How am I supposed to get to New York now?" he wondered aloud. He scrubbed his hand down his face and looked at the inferno in front of him.

The man who'd pulled him away looked at him as if he felt sorry for him, which was preposterous. He was the lord of the—oh, who was he kidding? Hades needed help. "Look, buddy," the man said, "I'm headed up to Portland. I gotta drive right through New York. I can give you a lift. But first, you need some regular clothes. You can't just go around like that."

"Like what?" Hades asked, wondering what was wrong with his attire.

"Like a *Rocky Horror Picture Show* reject," the man said.

Hades didn't know what that was, but he figured it wasn't good. Glancing around, he saw what the other people were wearing. "Okay, I'll be right back." He went into the store and found himself new clothes. This time he remembered to get comfortable shoes as well. After changing, he went back out to assess the damage.

"Son of a—my battle gear! My Helm of Darkness! Aphrodite's cloak! She's gonna *kill* me." Hades ran to the burned-out remains of his chariot. There was no way any of his gear survived. He had lost his helmet. He could no longer hide from eyes that would seek him out. He was screwed.

"I know, man," the man who saved him said. "I been there. Let's get going."

Hades hung his head and walked to the large truck. "I'm John," the man said.

"Hades," he grumbled back at him.

John nodded. "Interesting name, Hades. After the God of the Underworld?"

Hades considered correcting the man, but at this point, what was the use of it? Humans didn't believe in, much less fear the gods anymore. It would not help his situation at all to argue with the man who was taking him back to his wife. "Yeah, something like that," he answered him.

Just as the clerk from inside the store came running out, waving his arms at

Hades, he turned to John. "We should go. Now."

John started up the truck and put it in gear, leaving the flaming car and the clerk behind them.

***

He could see Persephone, standing in a wheat field. The grains grew to the height of her waist and she walked through it, brushing her hands across the tops of the long grass. She was walking away from him, her hair blowing in the gentle breeze. There was no way to describe the utter sense of relief that filled his heart. She was safe. "Persephone!" he called to her. She turned, and he saw her belly, swollen with child. "What is this?" he asked himself. Just as she would have come to him, the sky grew black and lightning flashed across the horizon.

"Hades!" she cried out to him.

Hades ran to her, but the harder he ran, the farther away she became. A dark figure rose up behind her, wrapping its shadowy arms around her. "Hades, help me!" He ran harder, desperate to get to her, but it was not fast enough. Maniacal laughter filled the air as thunder rolled over the mountains in the distance. He was taking her away! Hades pushed his legs harder, determined to get his wife back, when the shadow man consumed her. They winked out of existence before his eyes. She was gone. Lost to him forever.

***

Hades roared as he sat up straight. Where was he? Why was he confined in this tiny box? He smashed his fist against the glass, and it shattered into a million pieces. "Persephone!" he cried out.

"Whoa, buddy," a man's voice said. Hades turned to him, glaring. He seemed familiar. John. This was his chariot. "I think it's time you got out now." He pulled over to the side of the road and stopped.

"Are we in New York?" Hades asked.

"No," John answered. "But you've got a lot more psycho going on there, and I ain't taking any more chances with you. You broke my window!"

"You *will* take me to New York."

"If you don't get out, you're gonna have a twelve-gauge hole in your gut," John promised as he fetched his shotgun from beside the seat. Hades's first instinct was to bristle at the threat, but then again, he had very little power. He had been *dreaming.* Sleeping. He didn't need sleep, and yet he had done it. If that part of the curse was true, then perhaps so was the part about not being immortal. He would not look good with a hole in his middle.

The sound of the gun being cocked sealed the deal. "I will exit your chariot now," he said, opening the door and climbing out. No sooner than his feet touched the asphalt, did John speed away in his huge truck. As he stood there, alone and in the dark, Hades wondered what he was supposed to do now.

Chapter Eleven

Persephone twisted the golden ring around her middle finger. It wasn't that she was really looking at it, it was just a nervous habit that she'd formed over the course of a day or two. Her mind wandered increasingly often. She wondered where Hades was. What was he doing? Was he searching for her? Did he miss her? She wondered about what Sharalyn and Emma said about her curse. She was tied to Hades and she could never break her own curse if Hades's remained intact. The flutter of movement in her belly drew her line of thinking away from Hades and toward her child. He would be here soon, she could tell. Her belly had swollen to its maximum potential and the baby moved less every day. There was no more room for him to grow. Soon, he would be coming into the world, and she would be back on her way to the Underworld. The longer it took for Hades to come to his senses, the less likely it was for her to be free.

When someone knocked on the door, she didn't even look up.

"Why are you here?" Ares demanded.

"I want to help," a familiar feminine voice said.

Persephone turned to see who it was and got up from her seat on the sofa. "Hera?"

The goddess stood in the doorway wearing a fur coat and black slacks. She dressed like a human, but she still looked every bit the goddess she was. When she saw Persephone, she gasped and covered her mouth. "Oh, my," she finally said. "No wonder you ran from him." Then she turned to Ares. "I sent Hades here. Did he make it?"

"Yeah, he did," Ares growled. "We took care of it."

"I thought he wanted to take Persephone home. I had no idea she was pregnant!"

"Neither does he, and it stays that way."

"I want to help," she said sincerely. "The Goddess of Spring is one of the most powerful, kindest of our kind. She needs me."

"Let her in," Persephone said. Ares raised a brow but did as she said. He held the door open wide and allowed Hera entrance to his home. "Why do you want to help me?"

Hera glided into the house with her head held high and her back straight. Her strawberry-blonde hair cascaded around her delicately featured face. She appeared no older than thirty, but her eyes told the true story of how long she'd lived and what she'd lived through. Eons of knowledge, emotion, and stress were etched into her sapphire eyes. As she came through, she handed Ares her suitcase without so much as a "please" or "thank you."

"Hades came to us asking for our help," she said as she went to Persephone's side. "I told him to look here. He seemed worried for you. I had no idea that you were pregnant."

"I didn't want him to know," she said.

"And why would you? He's a selfish prick, just like his father. If I had known, I would have sent him away without so much as a 'piss off.''

"It's okay," Persephone said. "I need him to find me again and break his curse."

"That's right," Hera mused, "your curse is tied to his. A curse you never deserved if you ask me." She sat down on the plush sofa and crossed her legs. Persephone realized that everyone in the house was staring at the goddess. "But how will he break his curse?"

"Love is the answer," Persephone told her.

Hera sighed heavily. "There must be another way. Hades loves no one."

"I think it's time for you to go," Emma said to her.

"You heard her," Ares agreed.

Hera nodded. "I can see that I have not earned your trust yet. I understand. I will, in time." She patted Persephone on the knee and stood. "You rest and take care of yourself. I'll return tomorrow." And then, she left the same way as she arrived, regal as ever.

"I don't trust her," Emma said after she'd gone.

"No one does," Ares agreed. "She's up to something."

"I don't know, she seemed different," Poseidon said.

"Why are you still here?" Ares asked the god, exasperated.

Poseidon shrugged.

"You've *got* to talk to your wife," the God of War said with an exaggerated roll of his eyes.

Poseidon picked up the remote control and turned on the TV. "Who's up for some old reruns?"

***

Hades was sweating like a damned pig. The Lord of the Underworld did *not* sweat! Using the back of his arm, he wiped the salty moisture from his brow and cringed. Not only was he sweating, but his forehead was getting *sunburned*. It was late November, and it was *hot* outside. He knew it was, because his wife had not returned to the Underworld, and her mere presence on Earth was holding back the season change. Skadi, the Goddess of Winter, was probably getting pissed off by now. The females took turns, and Persephone wasn't playing by the rules. It wasn't unheard of for Skadi to seek vengeance on those who crossed her. If he didn't get Persephone back where she belonged and soon, the ice goddess would likely come for her.

He shoved down the sudden anxiety that filled his chest. His heart beat harder and his breath came in short pants. No, he couldn't allow that to happen. What was wrong with him? He was fearful, and not for himself. If he were completely honest with himself, he would say that he was afraid for Persephone's well-being. The urge to protect her at all costs was near overwhelming. And how, exactly, would he protect her? As much as he hated to admit it, Poseidon was right. He'd misused his powers and now they were damned near gone.

He studied his arms, noticing how dull they appeared, even in the bright sunlight. The godly glow had diminished. He looked like an over-sized human with a great sunburn. His hair was sticking to the back of his neck, increasing his discomfort and perspiration. Running his hands through it, he pulled it back and tied it in a knot behind his head. That allowed for a little breeze to brush across the back of his neck, and it helped to cool his overheated body somewhat.

The sun was high overhead, approaching midday. He knew he had to stay on this stretch of highway, but at the rate it was taking him to walk, he'd never make it to Persephone in time. He increased his pace to a jog and then to a run. There was nothing except the sound of his feet pounding against the pavement for a long time until he could run no more.

Hades fell to the ground in a heap, completely exhausted. He couldn't get enough air and his muscles screamed in pain. He tried to get up, but his body would not cooperate with his brain. So this was what it was like to be human, to have limitations, to be weak. Rolling to his back, Hades let the emotions he'd been holding back for so long come to the surface. He couldn't hold them back any longer. Physical pain dominated his body, but the mental pain was far worse. He'd failed. Everything his brother told him had been true. If he had only listened. He should have listened when Thanatos had tried to warn him, but he was too thick-headed. He'd used up all of his powers, lost his battle armor, and worse, he'd lost Persephone.

An image of her face flashed through his mind. Her long, dark hair swirling around her shoulders, her perfect, shy smile that she reserved just for him, her deep, sincere blue eyes. All of it. He remembered the day she'd been cursed to be his wife. He'd been a prick to her. She, of all the gods and goddesses, did not deserve the curse. She was everything pure and good with the universe, and Hades was not. He was selfish and cruel, arrogant, and petty. She gave life and love to the world. All she ever did was give and what, in all the time they'd been together, had he given her? Nothing.

And yet, somehow, she'd found something in him worth keeping. The first time she smiled at him, his whole Underworld lit up. The first time she laughed at one of his stupid jokes, it was like angels singing in his heart. The first time she'd come to his bed, he'd been so unsure. "Shut up and don't ruin it," she'd said to him. Hades made love to her that night, careful so as to not hurt her. He remembered as if it were yesterday the way her face relaxed, and she tilted back her head as she rode him. He remembered the sound of her breathing, the beating of her heart. He remembered it all.

And he'd taken it for granted. He assumed they would always be just as they were, trapped together in eternity. But Persephone was strong. So much stronger than he. She left him. She did the impossible

129

and defied her curse in search of freedom. She left him, and now he was lying on the side of the road, alone. He deserved no less. In fact, he deserved so much worse.

He had no way to protect her now. He had nothing. Going back to the Underworld to recharge was not an option. Even if he could, he would never get out again. The cloak and helmet were key in his escape and he'd lost those, too. Now, he would lose the woman he loved, and he deserved it.

As a single tear escaped his eye, Hades accepted his fate. He would die, right where he lay, on the deserted highway in the middle of nowhere. Alone and in pain, just as he deserved. He lifted his eyes to the heavens above him and made a plea for his wife. "God, I know I was an ass. I deserve everything I've got and more. Persephone does not. Please protect her. Give her everything she needs to live free of my curse and let her be happy." And then, he passed out.

Chapter Twelve

What is that infernal beeping! Hades opened his eyes, ready to smash whatever was making that horrid noise, when he realized he was not where he had been. He was lying in a tiny bed, nearly too small for his massive frame, with tubes and wires sticking out from all over. The light overhead was far too bright, and that beeping coincided with his heartbeat. What had happened?

"Good morning, sunshine," Poseidon's familiar voice said. "How's the head?"

Hades turned to look at his brother. "Fuck off."

"Yeah, so, I see your attitude has much improved." The Sea God chuckled. "You were found lying on the side of Interstate 81 just outside of Roanoke, Virginia. You were half-dead, dehydrated and had second-degree burns from the sun. Someone saw you, thought you were a corpse, called the police, and then realized you were still breathing. If that human hadn't called for help, you'd be dead now."

Hades glared at him. He should be dead now. Why did humans always have to interfere? "I didn't want to be saved."

"Good. Then I'm glad you were. There's hope for you yet."

"Are you insane?" Hades asked, sitting up and then wincing from the pain. "I have nothing left anymore. I have no reason to live."

"Why is that?"

Hades dropped back down and regretted it instantly when his back hit the pillow behind him. He kept his mouth closed and crossed his arms over his chest.

"You know, human psychiatrists say that crossing your arms like that is a defensive gesture. You have nothing to fear from me."

He was going to show his idiot brother a defensive gesture when he punched him in his stupid face. As he glared at the Sea God,

Hades hated him even more. Who looked like that? No wonder women had fallen at his feet for centuries. Why did he have to get the good hair, the great chin, the steely blue eyes? Hades had always hated him for it. Now, he realized that he didn't hate Poseidon, he was jealous. Not that he'd ever admit it to him or anyone else, and he was still gonna punch him for good measure. He realized that his brother was still talking.

"We need to get you back there because there isn't much time left. I was hoping you'd come to your senses before it was too late." He was saying.

"About what?"

"About your wife! Haven't you been listening?"

"No."

"No, you weren't listening, or no, you haven't come to your senses?"

"I wasn't listening. Look," Hades told him, "I might as well be human now. I can't go back, and I can't protect her. The best thing for Persephone now is to be as far away from me as possible."

"You love her."

Hades shrugged. "It doesn't matter. I don't deserve her, and she doesn't deserve my curse."

A huge grin spread across Poseidon's face, which made Hades want to punch him even more. "That's what I wanted to hear," the Sea God said. "Let's get you out of this mess." He moved faster than Hades's eyes could track, pulling all the plugs, wires, and tubes from his body. "Hmm, that little nightgown won't do, either," Poseidon said and then conjured clothes for Hades. "That's better."

Hades glanced down at himself and groaned. He was wearing soft denim pants that were too tight around his jewels, heavy black boots, and soft cotton T-shirt that was too damned small for his chest. "I look ridiculous," he said, already trying to find a new position for his cock. It was pinched in the tight pants, and he feared it may lose circulation.

"Trust me," Poseidon said, "you don't look ridiculous. Your wife is gonna have a hard time controlling herself when she sees you."

Persephone. His heart leapt in his chest. He missed her. "I told you, she doesn't need me."

"But she does," his brother told him. "She needs you now more than ever before and since you finally realize that you are nowhere near good enough for her, it's time to take you to her."

She needed him? How? Why? "Take me there."

Poseidon placed his hand on Hades's shoulder and ghosted them out of the hospital.

***

Her back hurt. Her legs hurt. Her hips hurt. Everything hurt, and all she wanted to do was eat pomegranates and barbeque. Persephone had refused assistance from Emma and Sharalyn. She wanted to be left alone. No, that wasn't exactly true. What she wanted was Hades. Over time, she'd come to love him and now that she was lying on the sofa, alone and in pain, she realized that he'd become her safe place, her rock. She missed him horribly and she just wanted him to hold her. She was afraid of the coming days. She was afraid of the curse, afraid for her baby, and afraid of childbirth. She had no doubt that she could do it, but the thought terrified her. So many things could go wrong.

She heard people talking in the kitchen and knew that Poseidon had returned. She couldn't hear the exact words, but she knew he'd found Hades. Rolling to her side, she managed to get herself upright and stood on shaky legs. She padded on bare feet to the kitchen, unable to fit into her shoes any longer due to the swelling of her ankles and feet. She moved much slower than she used to, but she managed to get there. And then, she saw him.

Hades was standing in the kitchen, his head hung low, staring at the floor. His massive shoulders had been stuffed into a light-green T-shirt that caressed his muscles like a lover. The color brought out the red in his hair, which was tied back in a messy, man-bun. She didn't think that she would have thought that was sexy, but right then, it was. His long, muscular legs were encased in a pair of snug blue jeans that left little to the imagination. Persephone's mouth went dry, and she wanted to climb up his body, kiss him from head to toe, then lick him all over like a—she really needed to get her hormones under control.

As if he could sense her standing there, he lifted his head and his brilliant green eyes met hers. Then he saw her. *Really* saw her.

His eyes traveled over her face, down her chest to her very, very pregnant belly. "Persephone," he breathed.

She waited for him to chastise her about keeping the baby a secret. Waited for him to let loose his anger over her disappearance. Waited for the fury that did not come.

He moved toward her slowly, looking her over again with each step he took. When he was directly in front of her and she was looking up into his eyes, he dropped to his knees in front of her. He circled her waist in his arms and laid his head upon her swollen belly. He didn't say anything, just held her. Persephone placed her hands on his head, feeling his body trembling against hers. He wasn't angry with her. In fact, he wasn't angry at anyone that she could tell.

He held her like that for a long moment before turning his face up to her. That's when Persephone lost control of her own emotions. Hades, the Lord of the Underworld, the biggest, baddest god she knew, had tears in his eyes. "I'm sorry. I didn't know. I was ignorant. I was stupid. I was—"

"Shhh." She interrupted him, stroking his hair. "I'm sorry, too. I should have told you."

"No, you shouldn't have," he said. "If you'd told me, I would have refused to let you leave alone. You would have never defied your curse. You don't deserve to be cursed. I do. I wish I could bear it for you, but that's not to be. I would do anything to take it away from you."

Persephone took his hands and said, "Come, sit with me. I find it's hard to stand for very long right now."

Hades stood to his full height of six feet seven inches, towering over Persephone. "You shall not have to stand another second." He scooped her up into his enormous arms and cradled her close to his body. He carried her into the living room where everyone else had gathered. "Where is your room?"

Persephone pointed toward the hall, and Hades carried her to her bed. "I missed you," she admitted as he laid her gently on the mattress.

He curled his body around her and pulled her to his chest. "I cannot describe to you what I have been through. Just know that I was a dick, I don't deserve you, and I will do everything I can in my limited power to protect you and our young."

"For now, just lay here with me and hold me." She sighed, feeling more relief than she had in months.

Chapter Thirteen

Persephone didn't know exactly when she'd drifted off to sleep, but she awoke to the feeling of Hades's lips on the side of her neck. He was brushing them softly against her skin, tasting her gently. Her skin broke out in gooseflesh and a delicious chill swept throughout her body. It had been so long since she'd felt his mouth on her and it felt wonderful. She turned her head slightly, allowing him greater access. He continued to kiss her, down her neck to her collarbone, then over her shoulder. His arm laid heavily over her side and belly, his hand tucked beneath her.

He continued his path back up her neck to her ear, where he nibbled at the lobe. Her eyes closed, and she sighed. "I missed you."

"I cannot tell you how I missed you," he rumbled against her skin. "How I've missed the scent of your hair and the taste of your skin. I've missed your smile and your grace. I've missed your beauty and your kindness."

Persephone turned so that she was on her back, her belly rising up like a mountain. "I wanted our baby to be born free."

"I know." His eyes were sad. "I'm sorry you had to go through this alone." He trailed his fingers over her belly, tracing invisible designs on the fabric of her shirt.

"It wasn't bad," she explained. "Then when I thought I would lose it, Ares found me. I met Emma and Sharalyn. These are good people."

"I know," he agreed. "Even my brother isn't so bad."

"I thought he was crazy," she admitted on a short laugh. "But he's crazy like a fox."

"Mhm." His hand had found its way under her shirt and he was touching her skin. "You're so beautiful," he told her. "I want— I need to touch you."

Persephone nodded and sat up. She pulled her shirt over her head, tossing it aside and then attempted to unlatch her bra. She couldn't quite reach it, but Hades was on top of it. With a flick of his wrist, the garment came loose, and she slid the straps off her arms. She hoped that he wouldn't be afraid of her new body, that he'd love it just as he had before. She needed his touch, too, and it had been too long.

When she laid back onto the pillows, Hades propped himself up on his elbow next to her. "My, these are different." He palmed her breast in one hand, clearly noticing how much bigger it was than before.

"They've grown a bit," she admitted.

Hades raised a playful brow at her, gave her a half-smile, then dropped his mouth over her nipple. The feel of his hot mouth on her delicate nipple sent electric waves straight to her core, and she arched her back. He sucked at her gently, released her, then lapped over the taut nipple with is tongue. Getting up onto his knees, he leaned over her body to pay the same attention to her other breast. She weaved her fingers through his hair, grasping tight and holding him to her body. She didn't want him to ever let go.

But he did let go, only to kiss a blazing path over her stomach and then back up again. He kissed and nipped at her neck, then along the line of her jaw. He cradled her face in his hand, rubbing his thumb over her cheek as he stared into her eyes.

Of all the times they'd had sex, nothing was as intimate as his stare right at that moment. She saw so many things reflected in his eyes. He feared. He was in pain. But most of all, he loved her. He didn't need to say it—it was written all over his features. Reaching up to take his face in her hands, she pulled it down to meet hers.

He kissed her mouth gently, sucking at her bottom lip, then tracing it with his tongue. When she opened for him, he slid his tongue inside her mouth. He kissed her with a passion that she had not known he was capable of, exploring her mouth as if it were the first and last time. He held her face in his hand, keeping her still while he took possession of her mouth.

When breathing became necessary, he let her go only to return to kissing her neck.

His hot breath bathed her skin, lighting her up from the inside out. He kissed over her belly, showing it the same amount of love that he'd shown the rest of her body so far. Then, he kissed her pelvis. Hooking his fingers under the band of the yoga pants she'd taken to wearing, he pulled them down her legs until she was free of them. He dropped a kiss on the top of her panties before ridding her of those as well.

When she was completely exposed to him, he stared at her for a long time. "So beautiful," he murmured. Hades positioned himself between her knees, bending them up on either side of his legs. He kissed her knee, then her thigh, swirling his tongue over her skin. He made his way up her leg until he was centered at her core.

As soon as his tongue touched her flesh, Persephone cried out.

"Am I hurting you?" he asked, raising his head.

"No," she answered, pushing his head back down. She needed him to keep going.

She was on fire and he was the only one who could put it out. Hades returned to his intimate kiss, licking and sucking at her clit until her legs shook uncontrollably. He reached over to her legs, lifting them and placing them over his shoulders so that she would not have to support them.

Then he pushed his arms under himself and added his fingers to the wonderful, delicious torture. Every swipe of his tongue was countered with a brush of his finger at her opening. Persephone needed more. Bucking her hips, she tried to tell him wordlessly what she wanted. He wasn't getting it, or he wasn't cooperating.

"I want you inside of me," she finally told him.

She felt more than heard his chuckle before he slid his finger into her. He crooked it slightly, hitting the exact spot where she needed the pressure. He sucked her clit into his mouth, and she shattered for him, bucking wildly against his mouth. He stayed with her until the tremors subsided, kissing and licking at her gently.

Then he rose up and wiped the moisture from his chin. "That was amazing."

"I thought so," she teased. "Why are you still dressed?"

Stark fear colored his face. "Oh, no, we can't. I would hurt you."

Persephone smiled sweetly at him. "I am not broken, and you will not hurt me."

"The baby," he countered.

"The baby is well protected within me. Naked. Now." She could tell he was still hesitant, but he would deny her nothing. She watched as he stood and then pulled the T-shirt over his head. His chest was every bit as amazing as she remembered, the muscles bulging with every move he made. He did, however, have an interesting tan line on each of his arms. He unfastened his jeans and pushed them down his legs, kicking them off. He stood in front of her in all of his naked glory, beautiful as ever. Her mouth began to water as the urge to taste him took over.

She rolled onto her knees and crawled to the edge of the bed where he stood. His cock jutted out from his groin, pointing at her as if it needed her as much as she needed it. The tip wept a little, and without giving him warning, she lapped up the drop of moisture.

"Fuck!" he groaned. "You don't have to—"

He stopped talking when she took him into her mouth. She tried to take him all the way in, but it just wasn't happening. His hands were in her hair, holding her but not trapping her. He allowed her to move freely, moaning encouragement and approval.

He finally insisted that she stop. "I need, I mean, if I can, I want—"

"Yes," she said, turning around so that she was on all fours and waiting for him.

"Fuck me," he groaned as he crawled on the bed behind her. On his knees, he guided himself to her entrance. She was slick and ready for him, but still, he hesitated. "Are you sure?"

She'd never been more positive about anything in her life. "Do it, now."

He pressed forward, entering her slowly. Persephone savored the feel of him filling her, pushing her to her limit before he slid back out again. "You okay?" he asked.

Instead of answering, she pushed her hips back, taking him inside of her again. His answering growl was good enough. He pushed into her slowly, again and again, lighting that fire inside of her once more. She could tell he was holding back, and that was not what she wanted. Raising up so that she was upright on her knees, she turned her head to see him.

He wrapped his arm over her chest and held her face as he kissed her lips. Then, he let her face go and used that hand to cup her sex as he moved harder and faster. His hold was firm, keeping her from falling over as he drove into her.

When his fingers began to dance over her clit, her body lit up, bucking back against him with fervor. "Persephone!" he called out her name as he held her tight.

There were so many emotions—she couldn't pin them all down—but at the moment, the biggest emotion was love. She loved him. At that moment, she had hope that they would see this through. For the first time since her journey began, the goddess believed that everything would be all right. As she came apart for him, Hades roared behind her, still crushing her to his body.

As they breathed heavily, recuperating, Hades kept her in his arms as he lay them both on the bed. He stayed curled around her, stroking her hair and kissing her shoulder as she came down from her orgasm-induced bliss. She ignored the way her belly had tightened, allowing herself to drift off to sleep in her husband's arms.

Chapter Fourteen

"Hey there, little jack rabbits," Poseidon said from the recliner when Persephone and Hades came out of their room.

Hades didn't say a word but shot a secretive smile to Persephone just before he pushed on the back of the recliner, using Poseidon's body weight to tip the chair over backward, sending the Sea God spiraling back with his feet in the air.

"I've wanted to do that for months," Ares admitted on a laugh. "Serves him right."

Poseidon flailed his arms and legs like a turtle on its back for a moment before ghosting himself upright. "That was low, Brother."

"Fuck you," Hades said, but it lacked his usual conviction. In fact, it sounded playful.

"Morning, guys," Emma said, bringing Hades a cup of hot coffee and a cup of hot tea for Persephone. "Did you guys get any curse breaking done last night?"

Persephone felt all of her blood rush to her face. "I, er, uh—"

Hades sheltered her under his arm and pulled her to his side. "I think we made some progress," he said with a wicked smile. "I'm not sure, exactly, how we're supposed to break it."

"Well," Emma said, sitting down on the sofa and sipping her coffee, "the key is love. I'm not sure how you go about it, but I know Ares was willing to keep his curse, to go back to Olympus forever, for my happiness."

Poseidon lifted the recliner upright and sat back in it. "I had to risk getting toasted for mine."

They explained to Hades how each of the gods had broken their curse. "In your curse, it says a selfless act. You gotta do something extreme for someone else." Emma set her cup on the coffee table. "I can't tell you who or what, just that you have to do it."

Hades shook his head. "I don't understand. I'm damn near powerless. I'm sunburned! I prayed for my wife. I was ready to die on that road, but still, there is more?"

"I guess so," Emma said, but the sound of a baby crying interrupted the conversation. "I'll get her."

Persephone smiled when Emma returned with baby Rhya in her arms. "May I?" she asked, holding her hands out.

"Of course," Emma said, handing the baby over to her.

Persephone peered down into the little one's sleepy eyes. She could hardly wait for her own child to come into the world. She loved this child so much already and she could only imagine how much she would love her own. When she felt Hades's eyes on her, she turned to him. He was staring at her with equal amounts of awe and terror. She glanced back at Emma, who nodded, and then back at her husband. "Want to hold her?" she asked him.

Hades shook his head and immediately began to back up. "Oh, no, that won't be necessary. I'll break her. I don't know how to, I can't—" Persephone smiled and handed the baby to him. He took her in his large hands, mostly because she didn't give him a choice. He held her out at arm's length, staring at the child with sheer terror. "Persephone," he pleaded, "I'm not comfortable with this. She's too small. I can't—I think you should take her back."

Emma intervened, but not to save Hades. She helped him hold the baby close to his chest. "Hold her like this. Let her head rest on your arm." She maneuvered Rhya until Hades had a better hold on her, then let go. "See, you can do it."

Persephone tried not to giggle, but it was damn hard. The big, bad, Lord of the Underworld was terrified of a demigod baby. It didn't take long, though, for him to soften up toward her. He looked into the baby's eyes and he smiled at her. When the baby cooed at him, he chuckled. "You are a pretty one," he told her. Soon he was swaying side to side, making faces at the infant and smiling like a damn fool.

"Crazy, isn't it?" Poseidon asked. "That insta-love that babies cause."

"It is," Hades agreed. "Okay, that's enough." He handed the baby back to her momma and turned to his wife. "We will have one of those."

Her heart filled with joy at his words. They would. They would have the baby together. They would be surrounded by their new family, and everything would be okay. She hoped. Speaking of which… "Where are Athena, Sharalyn, and the others?"

"They went home," Ares said with a pointed look at Poseidon. "They have homes to go to."

"Athena and Thor will be here later. Sharalyn and Thanatos are making sure the Underworld stays in order while you guys are away." Emma was feeding Rhya while sitting on the sofa. She had a blanket over her shoulder, but they knew that's what she was doing.

"That's very nice of them," Persephone said. Someone should be looking out for the Underworld, and who better than the God of Death and his reaper wife?

"That imbecile had better not let anyone out of Tartarus," Hades growled.

"Even if Thanatos wanted to, I sincerely doubt Sharalyn would allow it," Ares said. "She's a stickler for the rules."

"Good," Hades muttered. A sparkle on his wife's hand caught his attention. "What is that?"

"It was a gift from Freya," Persephone said. "It has helped to hide me from my curse. As long as I wear it, I don't feel the pull to return to the Underworld."

"You accepted a gift from a Norse?"

Persephone smiled. "Many things have changed since you were last on Earth."

Hades bristled. He didn't like Thor, and he didn't like Freya. Norsemen couldn't be trusted. Then again, he didn't like his own family either, so there was that.

Someone knocked at the front door, and Ares went to answer it. "Ladies, welcome. Hello, Mother."

Mother? Hades stood in time to see Aphrodite and Hera walk through the entryway. What was she doing there?

"Hades! I'm so glad you made it!" She ran to him and wrapped her arms around his neck.

"I'm sure you are," he mumbled. "If you knew exactly where Ares lived, why didn't you tell me?"

"You wouldn't have listened even if I had," she reminded him.

Hades grunted.

"Persephone!" Hera glided over to his wife, and Hades had to stifle a growl. He didn't want her anywhere in the same universe as Persephone. "You are glowing!"

"Hello, Hera," Persephone said calmly. Outwardly, she appeared to be nothing but gracious as Hera made over her and the coming baby, but Hades knew his wife better than he thought. He could tell by the way she wrung her hands and the way she absently rubbed her belly that she was very uncomfortable with it.

"Mother." Hades interrupted. "Again, what brings you here?"

"I want to help," she said. "Oh, what a lovely ring! May I see it?" She gestured to the ring Persephone wore for protection.

"Mom always did have a soft spot for the shiny things in life." Aphrodite sighed.

"I promise I'll give it right back," Hera continued.

Persephone glanced at Hades, who only shrugged, and then reluctantly removed the ring and handed it to Hera.

While Hera was ooo-ing and ahhh-ing over the ring, it became obvious Persephone was in physical pain. "What is it, love?" he asked her.

"The pull is back, stronger than before," she said through gritted teeth.

Hera gave the ring back, and Persephone put it on her finger immediately. The pain subsided, and she sighed heavily.

"We have to break this curse," Hades told her, taking her hand in his own.

"What can we do?" Aphrodite asked.

"I'm not sure there is anything you can do," Ares said. "We have it all pretty well covered."

"We will stay here until this is all over," Hera announced. "You may not need us right this minute, but the need will arise. Where is the extra bedroom?"

"I don't know," Ares started to say, but Emma chimed in.

"Last door at the end of the hall. I'll get you some extra bedding."

As the three women walked down the hall, Ares, Hades, and Poseidon exchanged uneasy glances. They wanted and needed all the help they could get, but at what cost? None of them truly trusted Hera or Aphrodite. For now, they would wait and see.

Chapter Fifteen

"I just don't like it, is all," Athena said after taking a sip of her coffee.

"I don't either," Emma admitted, "but we need help to figure out how to break this curse."

"I think we're trying too hard," Sharalyn said. "I think if we just hang tight, everything will work out like it's supposed to."

"Yes, but your mother isn't a lying bitch," Athena pointed out. "I'm surprised our mother didn't just eat us after we were born. Or toss us off the mountain."

"She doesn't seem the motherly type," Emma agreed. "The way she looks at Rhya gives me the creeps."

"Just don't leave her alone with Persephone," Athena said. "Let her help but keep one eye open."

"Right," Emma and Sharalyn agreed.

***

It was time. She had to act now. Hera tiptoed down the hall to Persephone's room. Hades was in the shower, and everyone else was outside talking over a campfire or some such nonsense. It was the only time she would get to be alone with the goddess.

Persephone was sleeping soundly on the bed, her hand hanging over the side as if she were waiting for Hera to come. The ring glinted in the dim light, beckoning her to it. Hera moved slowly, deliberately, to the bed and gently took the ring in her fingers. She carefully slid it off the goddess's hand and placed it in her pocket.

Persephone jerked in her sleep, and Hera raced out of the room just before the goddess screamed. Acting as if she had just arrived, Hera flung the door open wide and turned on the light. "What is it?"

"I can't," she cried, "The pain. I have to go. Now."

Hades slammed into the room. "What the hell?"

"The Underworld. It's calling her now. She must go there, or else she will surely die."

"The ring?" Hades asked.

"Is gone. I don't know where it is."

"We'll never get her there in time," Hades said. "Persephone, tell me what to do."

"I have to go," she cried. Her back arched, and she screamed.

"Somebody take her there!" he roared.

"I can help," Aphrodite said, running into the room. "I have used almost none of my power. I can ghost her there."

"Do it," Hera told her.

Aphrodite placed her hand on Persephone's shoulder and ghosted away.

"I have to get to her." Hades ran outside where Ares and Poseidon were. "Now. We have to go now!"

"Whoa," Poseidon said, holding out one hand. "What's going on?"

"Persephone! The ring—the Underworld! She's gone and I have to go with her!"

"Wait, what?" Ares barked, getting to his feet. He glanced at Emma and then at Hades. "Let's go."

There were no more questions asked—Poseidon and Ares ghosted Hades back to the entrance of the Underworld.

When they arrived, what they saw filled Hades with rage. Aphrodite and Hera were doing their damnedest to haul Persephone into the Underworld.

"You don't get to die and leave us in a winter wasteland!" Aphrodite was shouting.

"I did not escape from that mountain to live on a dead planet," Hera said. "Now, go willingly and have that baby in the Underworld like a good little goddess."

Persephone was fighting back, swinging her fists and kicking at the women, but her condition had left her significantly weaker than the goddesses.

"Unhand her!" Hades roared.

The women glanced up but continued to try to force the goddess into the entrance.

Ares jumped in and grabbed Aphrodite by the arm, throwing her into the trees.

"You wouldn't *dare* touch your mother," Hera snarled at Ares.

The God of War backed off for a moment, then grabbed Hera by the arm. "Don't make me hurt you," he warned.

"You wouldn't *dare*."

"I would." Ares gave her a pointed look and then nodded at her grip on Persephone. Hera, let go.

"Persephone!" Hades called out, running to her. "I'm so sorry."

"Back to Olympus with you," Ares said to his mother. "You got Aphrodite?"

"Got her," Poseidon said, holding their sister up by the back of her shirt.

The two gods disappeared with their cargo in tow, off to Olympus to trap them on the mountain once again.

Hades stared at his wife in his arms. She didn't look right at all. Her skin was pale, and she was sweating. "What can I do?"

"I think I am in labor," she said between breaths.

"Holy crap. Are you sure?" Hades's heart jumped into his throat and beat furiously.

"Pretty sure," Persephone said, cringing with pain.

Hades helped her to lie on the ground with her head on his lap. "Okay, what are we supposed to do here? Breathe?"

"I don't know!" Persephone screamed and curled in on herself. When the pain passed, she laid back against Hades, and that was when he saw the blood.

"Oh, fuck me! You're bleeding!"

Persephone stared down and saw a river of blood between her legs. "I don't think that's supposed to happen," she said before passing out.

"No, no, no! Ares! Poseidon! Get your asses back here!"

The gods appeared almost instantly. "We had to secure them—holy shit!" Ares barked. "We gotta get her inside." He moved as if to pull the goddess into the cave.

"No," Hades said. "She didn't come all this way to drop out now. She will kill us all if we take her in there. Eat us alive and pick her teeth with our bones!"

"That doesn't seem like Persephone," Poseidon said.

"Smartass. Hospital. *Now*!"

Chapter Sixteen

"I swear, you had better not even consider touching her," Hades growled at Thanatos. "I don't care what your little paper says."

"It's not a paper," Thanatos said, "it's a scroll, and you know I have no control over who's name appears on it."

Hades shook his head. He had never felt so… helpless before. Even though his brothers were by his side, free of their own curses, there was not enough magic to simply heal his wife. She'd used the very last of her power to try to defend herself from Hera and Aphrodite. Hades had none left, either. Ares and Poseidon had their power, but it wasn't a healing power. Nor was Thanatos's. In fact, that god's power was to kill.

"I'm not a killer," Thanatos said, as if he were reading Hades's mind. "You know very well that if I don't touch the dying, the entire balance is thrown off."

"I don't care. You'll *not* touch my wife!"

"I don't have a choice if her name——"

"Let's hope it doesn't come to that," Sharalyn said, placing her gloved hand on her husband's shoulder. "For now, let's hope the doctors can do their jobs."

Right on cue, the human doctor came through the double doors. He looked at the men sitting in his waiting room, shuffled his feet, stared at the ceiling, then at Sharalyn and Emma. He took a deep breath and looked up again. Had the situation been different, his reaction to the gods in the room would have been comical. Poseidon with his too-pretty face, Ares with his war braids and scars, Thanatos with his dark hair, clothes, and eyes that spoke of death, and Hades, who just appeared like a warrior straight out of a Scottish romance novel. It would be very intimidating.

The doctor finally screwed up his courage and came to them. "Are you the family of, uh, Persephone?"

"I am her husband," Hades said, standing.

The doctor backed up a couple of steps. "She is in labor; it seems a bit early. The baby is fully developed, but it's hard to say with no prior prenatal care. We have slowed it down, but we are unable to stop it. She will deliver today."

"This is good news, right?" Hades asked, a glimmer of hope growing inside of him.

The doctor didn't smile. Shouldn't he be smiling for good news?

"Your wife is bleeding much more than she should be. We are going to have to deliver the baby by cesarean section. It poses a great risk to your wife."

"No," Hades insisted.

"What are the options, doctor?" Emma asked, standing beside Hades and placing her hand on his arm.

"We really don't have any," the doctor admitted. "If we don't deliver and very soon, both mother and baby will be lost. Because of the blood loss, the amount of time it will take to save one will surely cost the life of the other. I wish I could say we could save them both, but I fear it's just not possible."

Fear. Anger. Rage. Sadness. Despair. All the things Hades didn't want to feel came crashing down on him at once. If this was what it was like to be human, he wanted no part of it. It was completely overwhelming, and Hades let it out on a roar that shook the walls. "I will see her now."

The doctor knew better than to argue. He nodded and turned for Hades to follow him. They traveled through a long hallway until the doctor stopped at a room enclosed by only a curtain. "We have only minutes," he said before pulling the curtain back to allow Hade's entrance.

His wife was lying on the small bed, her swollen belly covered by a thin sheet. "Persephone," he breathed.

She was awake. She turned her head to face him and smiled. "Hades. I was afraid you wouldn't be able to come back here."

"The doctor says you need an operation," he said, taking her hand.

Persephone nodded. "Soon."

"Please, don't do it," Hades begged. "We can make more babies. A hundred of them if you want. Please do not leave me." He knelt beside her bed and kissed her hand. "Don't leave me."

Persephone reached over to stroke his hair. "You will make sure our child has a good life."

"I can't do it without you," he said. "Please, do *not* leave me. Stay. Just a while longer."

"I have always loved you," she told him with a tear in her eye. "I love our baby. You take care of him."

"Him?"

"It is a boy." She smiled. "He will need his father."

"He needs his mother, too," Hades insisted. His chest was being crushed. His wife was saying goodbye. "Please don't go."

"It's time," a nurse said from the entrance.

Persephone nodded and squeezed Hades's hand. "It will be okay. You'll see."

"Persephone, no," Hades cried. The tears flowed freely down his cheeks. "I was a fool. I love you more than I could ever tell you. Stay with me. Please."

The nurse had come in and unlocked the brakes on the bed, preparing to push it out into the hall.

"I love you," Persephone said to Hades. "Always."

The nurse began moving the bed and Hades had to let go of his wife. He watched her go down the hall to the place where they would perform the operation. Another nurse came to him. "I'll take you back to the waiting area."

Hades followed her, a shell of who he was, broken and afraid. His Persephone. His goddess. How many years had he taken her for granted? How long had he been in love with her and was too stubborn to admit it? How much time had he wasted with her?

He went to the waiting room and sat in a chair, feeling the eyes of his family around him. He didn't dare look at them or to speak for fear of losing control of his emotions. That was not what Persephone needed. She needed him to be strong and it was taking everything he had to pretend to be.

After only a few minutes, a lullaby played over the intercom system and people clapped and cheered. A baby had been born. Someone was patting him on the back, and he turned. It was Thanatos. The god had a sad smile on his face. "Your baby is here."

"And you have to go now," Hades said sadly.

Thanatos nodded. "I'm sorry, brother. I am so very sorry."

Hades nodded. He knew the choice Persephone would make. She made it because she was so much stronger than he had ever been. She had so much more faith than he did. She was everything he was not. "Tell her I love her," Hades finally said.

Thanatos nodded and ghosted away to take Persephone to her afterlife.

Chapter Seventeen

In the distance, Hades heard a church bell ring. It was a mournful sound that signified the passing of not only his wife, but spring itself. Winter had begun. Winter would stay. His lovely Persephone had sacrificed everything for one child. Even though Hades was surrounded by people who cared, he had never felt so alone.

He wondered if Persephone would stay in the Elysian Fields, surrounded by her beloved flowers and beauty. Or would she choose to drink from the River Lethe and forget her former life, be born as a human and live another one? He hoped for the latter. He wanted her to have a happy life, not the one she'd had with him. He'd caused her nothing but angst. She deserved another life. A life without him.

"Hades," a too-familiar voice said.

He glanced up and saw the face of his nemesis, Thor. He couldn't even gather the strength to hate the fucker. "Thor."

"We came as soon as we heard." Athena was saying. "What's going on? Where is Thanatos?"

"Thanatos had a job to do," Ares told their sister. Hades was glad Ares had taken over the talking. He couldn't do it.

"What job could be more important than being here right now?" Thor asked. And then it dawned on the God of Thunder. "Oh, no."

"Persephone?" Athena asked, although she already knew the answer.

His family touched him, tried to hug him, hugged each other. Tears were in everyone's eyes as they mourned the loss of his goddess. She was so loved by all and he didn't think she even realized it.

"Sir?" A nurse approached him.

Hades just stared at her.

"Please come with me."

Hades followed her to a regular room that had a crib and a rocking chair in it.

"Wait here," the nurse said.

Hades watched her leave. He felt like he was having an out of body experience of some sort. Life was continuing around him, but he was just along for the ride. He felt like a third-party looking in. None of it mattered anymore. None of it.

The nurse returned with a bundle of blankets in her arms. "Meet your son," she said, motioning for Hades to sit in the rocking chair. When he was seated, she placed the bundle in his arms. "He weighs eight pounds exactly," she said, pulling the blanket back to expose the baby's face. "We had to give him blood immediately, but otherwise he is healthy."

Hades peered down into his son's sleeping face. He looked so much like his mother. "I'll leave you alone now, but if you need us, just push this button." She pointed to a red button on the wall. "I am so sorry for your loss," she said before stealing out of the room.

Could he love this child that had taken his Persephone from him? Could he raise it without her?

One look into the baby's cobalt-blue eyes and Hades knew. He just knew. He loved the child. The feeling was powerful and damned near overwhelming. It filled his heart and threatened to break free—there was so much of it. He knew he could love the baby his wife loved so much without ever having met. He also knew there was no way he could give the child the life he deserved, and there was no way he could make an attempt at it without Persephone. She was everything light, and he was dark. She was the embodiment of life itself, while he was death and destruction. How could he subject the little one to the Underworld? How could he make that choice? He couldn't.

His chest felt as if the weight of the world rested upon it, while his heart broke in his chest. Persephone had not lived. There was no hope to find there. Only pity for Hades and his newborn son that were doomed to an eternity of darkness and death.

It became too much to bear and Hades wept with his son in his arms. The little one weighed next to nothing, but the weight of his responsibility was overwhelming. Who would teach him to forgive? Who would teach him reason? Who would teach him love? The Lord of the Underworld? No. Hades had only just discovered those things himself and couldn't possibly teach the child that.

His shoulders shook with the power of his cries, and soon, the grief found a voice. Hades cried out to the heavens, to the universe, in the unfairness of it all. He roared with grief and frustration, feeling the last of his powers leave his body. He felt weak. Vulnerable. And for the first time, truly afraid. Not for himself—but for the tiny baby that rested in his arms.

"God, I don't know if you can hear me, or if you even care. I don't know where else to turn. This tiny one has done nothing to deserve your wrath. He has done nothing to deserve a life of death. Please, let his mother live. I'll do anything. I'll say anything. I'll give up anything to let her be with him. She defied you to bring him into this world. I don't care about power, or the Underworld, I only care about the little one. Take me instead. I will take her place but let her live!"

He didn't know what he expected to happen. It surely wasn't Ares coming in the room. "Hey, Bro, how are you holding up?"

Hades's shoulders slumped. "Not well," he answered honestly.

"Sometimes things don't work the way we expect them to," Ares said, holding his hands out to Hades. "Can I hold him?"

Hades nodded, handing the baby to Ares. "He looks like Persephone."

"Yes," Hades agreed. "He does. I wish she could know her."

"Me too, brother."

Hades watched Ares, the God of War, sway and coo at the tiny baby. The warrior had grown into a father, and a damned good one at that. Hades wished that he could be like that. He wished for many things. Mostly, he wished a good life for his son. And then, it occurred to him. "You are a good father," he said.

"Thank you," Ares said. "And you will be, too."

"And being a good father means making hard choices."

"Sometimes." Ares nodded.

"We must always do what is best for our children."

"Yep."

"Our parents sucked."

Ares chuckled. "Yeah, pretty much."

"You will raise him."

Ares raised a brow at Hades but said nothing.

"You are a good, loving, forgiving man who is strong enough to teach my son not only how to fight and be strong, but how to love, too. I do not possess the strength to do this for him. I must return to the Underworld, a place I do not want my son to grow up. You will raise him. You and your lovely wife. He will have a good family.”

“What about you? You need a family, too.”

“You are my family, and one day we shall find a way, but for now, my son will have a life without me. Without his mother. You will raise him.”
Ares pressed his lips together and clearly fought the tears that threatened to spill over. “It would be my honor to raise and protect your son.”

“Thank you,” Hades said sadly.

“What have you named him?”

“I haven’t yet.”

“He needs a name and only you can give it,” Ares said.

Hades thought for a moment. “Amare.”

“Love,” Ares said in English.

"Yes." Hades inclined his head. "Because I have never loved anything more."

The light in the room flickered and Ares stepped back, holding the baby close to his chest. A bright-white light filled the room, emanating from Hades. Bathed in the light, he rose from the chair, his feet lifting from the floor as the light surrounded him. His red hair caught fire and the power he had lost filled him once again. He could feel it coursing through his veins, filling every cell with his powers.

When the light died down, Hades stood there, the god he'd always been.

"Does this mean my curse is broken?" Hades asked.

Ares nodded.

"And yet, I don't feel like a god. I feel broken."

"I know," Ares said.

"I must return to the Underworld now," Hades told his brother. "Take care of Amare. I'll be back to see him."

"I would hope so. I will look after him until you're ready."

Hades nodded. He opened the door and stepped into the hallway.

"Are you going to ghost there?" Ares asked.

Hades's shoulders slumped. "I thought I'd walk."

"Put your hair out first," Ares said with a chuckle.

Hades smiled a sad smile and put his hair out. "Keep him safe."

Hades walked down the hall, past the nurse's station. He noticed a vase of dying flowers on the desk. This was how it would be from now on. No more flowers. No more grass. No more spring. He strode through the waiting room and out the front door. He had a job to do now. Amare would be safe with Ares and Emma. He would have a good life.

He walked away, prepared for the long, lonely life he had ahead. He didn't see the people who stared at him, he didn't see the traffic pass him by. He didn't see the sun in the sky, and he didn't see those flowers on the nurse's desk come back to life.

Epilogue

One week. Seven days. One hundred and sixty-eight hours. That was how long it had been since Persephone died. Hades had hoped that in her afterlife, Persephone would have come to the palace to see him, to let him know that she was okay. She had not. He debated on going out to find her spirit, but he restrained himself. Why would she want to see him? It was because of him that she'd died in the first place. If he had been a better husband, a better man, perhaps she wouldn't have run.

Would've, should've, could've. It didn't matter anymore. He was alone, just as he deserved to be.

Sitting on his throne, Hades went through the motions. He dictated who got what treatment in Tartarus, but really, he went along with whatever his servants wanted. He no longer cared about torture and damnation. All he loved was lost to him.

"Hades," Thanatos exclaimed, ghosting into the throne room. "You have to come with me."

"No, thank you," Hades said, looking away from the God of Death. He knew that it was his job, but he couldn't help but to hold a bit of a grudge against Thanatos for taking Persephone when she passed.

"I'm *serious*. Amare needs you."

"What?" Hades barked. "I told that brother of mine to take care of him! What has the imbecile done now?"

"You have to come and see."

"Lead the way." With his curse broken, Hades could ghost in and out of the Underworld freely, without need of his cloak or helm.

He followed Thanatos to Ares's house and barged right in. "What have you done?" he demanded.

"Whoa, big fella," Ares said. "Put your hair out and listen a minute."

"I want answers! Where is my son?"

"Your son is sleeping," the sweetest voice in the world said. Hades's anger cooled immediately as his wife walked into the room. "And I will be upset if you wake him."

"Persephone," he breathed. "Is it you? Truly?"

His goddess smiled and the whole world lit up. The birds sang outside; the sun shone a little brighter. The weight on his chest lifted and he ran to her, scooping her into his arms. "How is this possible?" he asked into her hair. "You were dead."

"I was," she said against his chest. "I can't breathe."

"Oh, sorry." Hades set her on her feet, then dropped to his knees in front of her. "You live."

"Yes. When you gave up our son for a life you couldn't give him, you made a sacrifice. A selfless act. You broke your curse, and in turn, broke mine."

"But how? Why now? How long have you been here?"

"It took a couple of days for me to come back. I was in the fields, and then I was yanked back here. I found myself at the hospital. The guy in the morgue was effectively freaked out. Anyway, we've been trying to get you here for days."

"I am so sorry, my love. I will never leave your side again. I swear it to you."

"You better not," she said. "Now stand up and kiss me."

Hades did as he was told. The unbearable weight he'd carried was lifted away, and for once in his long, pitiful life, all was right in the world. He knew how precious life and love could be, and he vowed not only to his family, but to himself, that he would never forget it again.

The End.

Bound in love, bound in hate

Until the bonds dissolve in fate

A life to give more precious than your own

A decision that will change the status quo

A prisoner to the afterlife you'll always be

A selfless act shall set you free

Bound to one cursed by fate

For a time an unwilling mate

The gift of life you shall give

Uncursed the new one will live

Bring forth the love he does not see

Opening his heart shall set you free

Thank you for reading Lord of the Underworld. If this is your first encounter with the Curse of the Gods, please check out the previous books in the series:

God of War: The God of War has a curse to overcome. Will Emma be the key to setting him free or will she be his undoing? Ares had been cursed to spend eternity on Mount Olympus, away from Earth and away from humans. The God of War did not give acquiescence easily, though and escaped only to find himself on an Earth like he had never known. Humans no longer believed in the Gods of Olympus, much less feared them. As time goes by, Ares finds that his powers, along with his immortality, are growing weaker by the day. Can one human woman help him to break his curse and overcome the war within himself?

Kiss of Death: Thanatos, god of death, had been cursed to never touch a living human. To do so would take the life of that soul. He performed his duties, taking the dead to the underworld, without a hitch until one woman got away. She was dead for five minutes. Her life had been saved, but not before touching Thanatos's hand. Now she is immune to his deadly touch and he can't get her out of his mind.

Could she be the answer to breaking his   curse?

Or will she be his kiss of death?

Legends and Heroes: Written with the incredible Angela Sanders: Greek and Norse mythology clash in the War of the Gods...

War raged for centuries between the Olympian and Norse Gods. However, when the Olympians were cursed by the Creator for their greed and pettiness, the conflict began to fizzle and was eventually forgotten. Until the day Loki, the Trickster, ran into Ares on Earth. Set on rekindling the war, he went to the God of Thunder and weaved a tale of lies and deception. Thor set out to seek vengeance on Olympus and that is where he saw Athena after centuries past.

Tensions run high as a web of lies brings the Norsemen and Olympians head to head, and war becomes imminent.

Athena has a curse to break and

she's been running from it for too long. Could this man, this Norse God of Thunder, be the key to setting her free? Will their unlikely alliance be strong enough to overcome centuries of hate and misconceptions?

Along with a few friends, allies in battle, they will fight for each other and the ones they love in this comedic heart pounding mashup romance.